CROSS BONES

Tracy Whitwell was born, brought up and educated in the North-East of England. She wrote plays and short stories from an early age, then in the nineties moved to London where she became a busy actress on stage and screen.

After having her son, she wound down the acting to concentrate on writing full time. Many projects followed until she finally found the courage to write her first novel, *The Accidental Medium* – a work of fiction based on a whole heap of crazy truth.

Today, Tracy lives in north London with her son, and has written quite a stack of novels. She is nothing like her lead character Tanz in the Accidental Medium series. (This is a lie.)

More by the author

Adventures of an Accidental Medium series
The Accidental Medium
Gin Palace

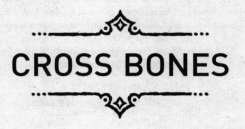

CROSS BONES

TRACY WHITWELL

PAN BOOKS

First published 2024 by Pan Books
an imprint of Pan Macmillan
The Smithson, 6 Briset Street, London EC1M 5NR
EU representative: Macmillan Publishers Ireland Ltd, 1st Floor,
The Liffey Trust Centre, 117–126 Sheriff Street Upper,
Dublin 1, D01 YC43
Associated companies throughout the world
www.panmacmillan.com

ISBN 978-1-5290-8758-1

1 3 5 7 9 8 6 4 2

A CIP catalogue record for this book is available from the British Library

Typeset in Stempel Garamond by Jouve (UK), Milton Keynes
Printed and bound by CPI Group (UK) Ltd, Croydon, CR0 4YY

Visit **www.panmacmillan.com** to read more about all our books
and to buy them. You will also find features, author interviews and
news of any author events, and you can sign up for e-newsletters
so that you're always first to hear about our new releases.

For Mandasue Heller, a life-changing witchy sister.

And for the outcast dead at Cross Bones.
Always remembered.

PROLOGUE

It's still day. Well, I think it's day, but the sky is a strange yellow colour I've never seen before and it's drizzling miserably. I draw in a breath, but it's shallow and it hurts my chest. My hands, *flippin' heck*, they've got veins like ropes and there are liver spots. They're an old man's hands and I'm holding a shovel; it's heavy and I'm digging it into mud that's becoming slimy. Then the stench hits me: Jesus, it stinks. It's fetid. I look round to see where the smell might be coming from as my old man's hands push the shovel hard into the soft ground, and I see a muddy turnip plop out right next to my feet. There are a few of these turnips and . . . *what's that?* Weird lumps of meat. Then I notice the meat has fingers and the turnips are made of bone – they're skulls, skulls lying about the place, with flesh and maggots everywhere.

Before I can scream, I'm in a little dark room. There's a tiny open fire, which is burning low with no heat. I can make out a window. There's a rag hanging in front of it and there's very little light. Again, it reeks. This time it's urine,

and something worse. There's a metal cup of some sort grasped in my veiny hand, with watery-looking tea in it. I hear coughing, distant persistent coughing, and I see the cup fall from my hand. It hits the sawdust on the floor with a far-off thunk. The coughing is becoming a wheeze. Then there's the sound of a woman screaming, desperate cries: *'You pulled him back out – my boy, my lovely boy, out of the ground . . . Why would you? Why?'*

Then the room darkens further, and suddenly the floor whooshes towards me and I open my eyes.

Sheila is holding my hand and we're sitting on a bench overlooking the concreted ground and a little garden plot. The sun is trying really hard to peek out from behind the clouds. It's so nice to escape the stink and breathe fresh air again.

'You all right, love?'

'Fucking hell, Sheila. I think I just died.'

SCOTLAND?

Elsa, my friend — my shallow, beautiful, fashion-crazy, Londonista journalista friend — has just shocked the life out of me. We're sitting in Minnie's, our favourite Crouch End bolthole, with a bottle of wine between us and a bowl of skin-on fries, because some arsehole made the rule that you must eat something to order alcohol here, which is frankly outrageous and an infringement on my human rights.

'You're moving?'

Elsa nods. She's wearing a chic dark-grey cowl-neck jumper dress with a jacket that probably cost more than my parents' house. She'll have bought it on her credit card, like it was nothing, and will soon have to open another credit card to help pay this one off.

'Tanz, I can't do this any more. My rent in the new place will be eight hundred pounds a month cheaper than where I am now.'

'But *Scotland*?'

'If I'm working for this new magazine there'll be

opportunities for me to blag my way into other commissions for other bigger mags later on. But I need to be there. I need to attend everything I'm asked to attend. Parties, drinks, book launches in people's living rooms – I don't care. I'm going to schmooze the hell out of the lot. And my flat will be ten minutes from anywhere I might be invited to, so I can be in bed before midnight, but if I want to stay out late, I'll always be minutes from home in a taxi. I'm knackered, Tanz. Right now I'm a tiny fish in a pond the size of, well, London.'

I can't help laughing; Elsa might be flaky, but she's very funny.

'I'm constantly running to catch up with money. I could live well there on the wage they're offering, and start paying off my cards. I have a couple of old friends from sixth form living in the area too, who are dying for my sophisticated London wit to light up their lives. Being here seemed the only sensible option after journalism school, but I've got to say, ten years on, I'm in my thirties, I'm single, I'm tired, I'm getting worry lines and I want a dog.'

'Since when did you want a dog?'

'I was brought up a half-country girl living on the outskirts of town. I always had dogs. I even had a horse. Something has switched in me. That last time I was mugged, I couldn't shake it off. I just started thinking, *This is too much*. Then that ghost in my house. I love that you and Sheila cleared her away. Poor old woman. But I started imagining myself, getting older and more bitter, like a lemon left at the back of the fridge. What if I cling on with my fingernails to my "London life" for ever and end up dead in the bathroom, my only hobbies for the past forty years being expensive wine and criticizing other people? I could end up being that old woman!'

I have never heard Elsa speak like this. It's disconcerting.

'When do you go?'

'Four weeks.'

'What the fuck? Four weeks?'

'You can come and stay whenever you like. It's a two-bed.'

As she speaks, the waiter walks past, a serious-looking Italian man, grey at the temples with a pencil behind his ear. I used to have an eye for the waiters, especially the gorgeous Irish one who worked in here, but I seem to have lost my appetite for flirtation recently. Elsa clocks my glance and looks at me curiously.

'Do you still miss Pat?'

I shake my head and force a smile.

'Not much.'

The truth is, after the ghostly shenanigans in Newcastle, playing that generic slut in *Penshaw Investigates* and then Caroline May dying so tragically, I've really fought off missing Pat. I got back a few weeks ago and I want a cuddle and a snog and for someone to say I'm beautiful. But it's not going to happen; Pat's travelling the world, meeting gorgeous lasses on the way – the slags – and I'm too old for him, to boot. So, sod it.

Elsa pats my hand.

'I don't believe you. But anyway today's about me and my new job. Me, me, me. Let's get another bottle!'

I know this won't end well, but hey-ho.

POLICE-CHILD

My eyes feel like half-fried eggs. What the hell was I doing moving on to that second bottle? The chips were all I'd had to eat since breakfast. I mean, it's the first rule of booze: don't drink on an empty stomach. A few bits of mangled potato were never going to cut it. I've now driven to St Albans and parked my car near the cathedral, after waking up late and sweaty and having the longest shower known to man. It accidentally started off as a freezing-cold shower, which elicited such a loud scream that I think I gave my Inka a feline heart attack. But then it warmed up and I just stood there, letting streams of tepid water patter off my hungover skin, wondering why I'm such a wine-greedy fool.

I check the parking meter: I have ninety minutes. I wash down two paracetamol with water from my favourite sky-blue metallic bottle, because there's currently a needle-sharp pain right in the centre of my forehead, shooting back into the middle of my brain. *Idiot!*

Neil the policeman is in Café Rouge. I've forgotten what

he looks like, and I flap about, looking hither and thither like a complete loser until at last I spot him waving and it comes back to me: boyish little face, unruly fringe that he probably tries to smooth down but can't, innocent-looking dark eyes that truly do make him look twelve. He's not dressed as a policeman today. He's in a sweater and black jeans. Seeing him suddenly brings back memories of Creepy Dan the Creepy Murderer, and the day Sheila and I were nearly toast at the hands of a deranged short-arse who resembled a bloodhound. My heart skips. It was very stressful.

Neil stands.

'Hey, Tanz. You look . . . tired.'

I can't help but laugh. It hurts my head when I do.

'I am so-o-o hungover, Neil. I'm sorry.'

'Sit down, let's get you right again. Lunch is on me, I'll sort this.'

Before very long he has their posh version of fish and chips in front of him and I have a full English, a great big filter coffee and an orange juice, as well as a jug of water. Neil orders extra toast for me.

'Butter that toast and get it down you, with all the proteins. Eat everything and have the orange juice for the sugar. The caffeine will help but have water as well – you're dehydrated.'

'Bloody hell, Neil. I'd say you were like my dad, but my dad wouldn't have a clue, as he doesn't really drink. You're an expert.'

He's not really an expert, since that lot could send me

7

straight to sleep and the caffeine could go either way, but I'll let him have his moment.

'Can't go to work on a hangover. Happens to the best of us, and you have to know how to solve it fast. It's that or a big bag of cheese and onion crisps and a fat Coke.'

Can't deny it: ten minutes later I'm feeling a whole lot better.

'I'm sorry to take so long to come and see you. I've felt a bit weird since I drove back from Newcastle.'

He shrugs. 'Of course you have. Your friend died.'

The death of Caroline May was big news for about a week. They rustled together a commemorative hour-long TV show about her life, which aired a fortnight ago. What a wonderful woman and great actress, yadda yadda yadda. The truth is she was complicated, drank too much and was a bitch to almost everyone. And in the very short time I knew Caroline – pathetic as it sounds – I grew to love her. It's not something I want to talk about, though; it makes me feel dizzy even thinking about it. She called me after she died. Not exactly something you can drop into the conversation.

'Yes. My friend died, and now my other friend is moving to the other end of the UK, hence us getting drunk last night.'

'Was it something you said?'

Neil's unexpected joke almost makes me suck coffee up my nose.

'You cheeky so-and-so. I'm a wonderful person, and it's not my fault that everyone I care about dies, moves away or goes travelling.'

I didn't mean to say that last bit, it slipped out. Neil nods his boyish head and thankfully doesn't ask who went travelling.

'You've only got about an hour on your meter left, haven't you? I'd better tell you about my mate.'

'God, of course. Your policeman-on-the-Met mate.'

'Yes. I, erm, I may have misled you a tiny bit about what he wants.'

Oh, now this is interesting: this police-child has been lying to me.

'Go on . . .'

'Okay, so my pal, Charlie, he does work for the Met and he loves the thought of using you on cases they're having trouble with – he's really into that spooky stuff. But he, well, he has a more personal case he wants to ask you about. It's his sister; she went missing on a street in Borough years ago. Never seen again. Her boyfriend lived in a flat off the high street. He said she left his at eight p.m. CCTV spotted her in a local corner shop, then that's it. Charlie wondered if you'd go there and stand near the boyfriend's flat and walk to the corner shop. He knows it's a long shot, and how mad it would sound to . . . well, lots of "normal" people.'

'Normal rather than weirdos like me, you mean?'

'Yes, that's right.' Neil grins.

'Anyway he said he'd come with you and walk you through it. Or if you're not willing, can he just talk to you? It's killing him not knowing. She was a complicated girl apparently, but he really loved her.'

'That's actually really sweet of you, Neil, trying to help

your friend like that. Of course, I'll give it a go. But I must tell you, there are no guarantees, because my supposed gift is as erratic as my work life.'

'Yeah. I can imagine being an actress is a bit dicey; all that worrying about money between jobs. But at least you're not boring, like me.'

'You're actually far less boring than I thought you'd be.'

'Cheeky moo.' Neil picks up the menu and looks at the drinks. 'What did you get drunk on last night?'

'White wine. And then champagne. That neither of us could afford.'

'Typical that you'd have expensive tastes.'

Before I can stop him, he's located fizz by the glass and has ordered me one.

'The last piece of the cure. Have a bit of whatever you had the night before. I know you're driving, so it's only one flute.'

'Bloody hell, police-boy, you sail close to the wind.'

'Enough of the "boy". I'm thirty-five years old, the Dorian Gray of St Albans. The Hertfordshire heartthrob.'

I'm shocked. We're much closer in age than I imagined. And my hangover has already diminished enormously. Every day's a school day.

SHIT FRINGE

As usual, the A406 is rammed as I drive back to my flat. I feel pleasantly woozy from that big fat meal and flute of fizz, and I put on one of my driving compilations – one with fewer filthy guitars than usual. I decide that ELO are the perfect happy accompaniment for the drive home, ready to get straight back into bed and sleep off the rest of last night. Typically, as I'm harmonizing with my favourite bit, the phone rings.

My ear wires are already plugged into the phone, a recently acquired state of paranoia mixed with ongoing poverty (yes, I just earned enough to cover the next four months of rent but, believe me, that is a *novelty*) meaning I'm determined never to get a fine for using my phone in the car. I saw that happen to someone else on the motorway – all flashing lights and being stopped on the hard shoulder. I mean, you can get *killed by lorries* when you stop on the hard shoulder. I also use wires now instead of my Matrix-like Bluetooth earpiece, as it used to fly out of my ear at inopportune moments, which was a fucker.

The minute I answer, the big voice of my agent Bill booms at me.

'Hello, Tanz! You've got a straight offer. Fringe play, but it's at the Old Red Lion. Easy to get to. Equity minimum, put you on that stage again, bring in some good casting agents. It's a lead. Great part. They liked you in that *Gently Does It* TV show you did a couple of years back.'

I'm less of a fan of acting onstage than I used to be. Laziness as much as anything, but also the stress, if the show's not great.

'Is it a good play?'

'No idea, darl'. Have a look tonight and get back to me.'

'Okay. What if I hate it?'

'Well, it's not like you've got anything else on. I mean, if you really hate it, then we can talk, but this is London fringe, so, you know . . .'

'Okay. You think it's a good idea, though?' I don't know why I'm asking this. I'll just be winding him up. He takes a patient breath.

'Of course. We need to get your profile out there as a stage actress. Have a read and tell me what you think. It's a great opportunity.'

'Okay, thanks. I'll call you when I've read it.'

I'll be fine once I'm home and my laptop's open, I'm sure of it. I'm only being awkward because I'm tired.

FERAL HORSE

I recently purchased a onesie. It's dark blue and velvety, with a hood and big silver stars all over it. I love putting it on and snuggling in front of the TV or lounging on the sofa with a book. Right now, I'm in my favourite armchair in my onesie, balancing the laptop on the arm of the chair, because Inka has insisted on curling up in my lap. My candles are lit and it's cosy but, as I feared, I really can't get my head around the play. I don't like the writing and it all seems a bit pretentious. Not knowing what to do, I call for Frank, my beautiful friend who died in a car crash a few years ago and broke my flippin' heart. He won't tell me what he does when he's not inside my head, taking the piss out of me, but nowadays I definitely don't get to chat to him as much as I did when I first discovered he was still 'with' me. Tonight, though – miracle of miracles – I feel his presence as soon as I say his name.

'Hola! Whoa, what are you wearing?'

'A onesie. They're the most comfortable things you can put on, and they save on heating bills. They're so toasty.'

'*But how do you go to the loo?*'

'None of your business. How are you?'

'*I'm fine. Saw you flirting with that copper today.*'

'I wasn't bloody flirting. I was trying to keep my lunch down; I was extremely hungover.'

'*Yes, you did cane it last night.*'

'Hey, if you're around watching all of this, how come you never pipe up?'

'*I'm omnipotent. I can watch you and still do loads of other stuff.*'

'Oh, so you're God now?'

'*We both always knew I was.*'

I snort, and Inka opens one eye and looks up at me inquisitively. I'm pretty sure my own cat thinks I've lost it.

'Anyway, I called you here for a reason. I've . . . well, I got offered a job and I don't really fancy it. I don't like the script that much.'

'*So don't do it.*'

'It would mean another few months of my rent paid, though, if I'm really careful. And Bill says it'll lift my theatre profile.'

'*So get on with it.*'

'I just feel odd about everything.'

'*Go to the audition and if you're still not sure, then maybe give this one a miss? To be honest, you'll have other fish to fry soon.*'

'There is no audition, it's an offer. And what do you mean by "other fish to fry"?'

'*Secret.*'

'Oh, come on . . .'

'*Let's call it your next adventure. Oh, and tell Milo congratulations from me.*'

'Congratulations for what?'

'*Byeeee.*'

'Oh, you dick!'

Gone. I stroke Inka's silky head and decide to take a ten-minute break from the play and call that Charlie fella, Neil's mate. Maybe looking into what happened to his sister will be my next 'adventure'. I'm not sure what else it could be. I grab my phone and, as I do so, it lights up and rings. I get such a fright that I nearly hurl it across the room. It's Milo. He's placing a video call; he doesn't do that ever.

I answer immediately, patting my hair down as I do so.

'Hiyaaaa.'

Milo's sitting at his desk, one side of his face lit by a lamp, his eyes sparkling. That cheeky smile is extra naughty today. What's he been up to?

'Hello, my little darlin'. I hear congratulations are in order,' I say to him.

He cocks his head. 'You *what*? How did you—'

I realize I've just stolen Milo's thunder. Oops.

'I'm sorry – I was talking to Frank and he said to tell you congratulations from him.'

Milo rolls his eyes.

'You know what, I don't care if he's dead; he's got no right deflating my sails like that, the bloody spragger.'

'He didn't tell me what. Honest.'

Milo sniffs and recomposes himself.

'Right, still . . . Anyway, yes. I've had some good news.'

'Come on then, Milo, spill.'

'Channel Four are finally making that one-hour film I wrote. It's in a series of five one-offs. I've got a list of edits to do that's longer than the Lambton Worm, but it pays well, so I'll not be shitting myself about money for a bit. I feel like doing a dance!'

'Oh my God, that is so great. *Congratulations*. And do it! I want to see you dance.'

Suddenly Milo stares hard at the phone screen.

'What the fuck are you wearing?'

'It's a onesie. It's got stars on it.'

'Fuck, I think I want one. Is that a hood?'

'It is.'

'It's so vile it's almost wonderful.'

'Oi! It's the cosiest thing in existence.'

Milo runs his hand through his currently spiky thatch and looks thoughtfully into the screen again.

'Tanz, despite my fabulous state of mind as a newly hatched top TV writer, I can't help noticing you seem a bit off.'

'What?'

'I video called so I could see your canny face when I told you my news. The news Frank spoiled, the wanker. But there's something else going on in that brain of yours. I can tell. Your eyes are glinting like a feral horse's.'

'Isn't it me who's supposed to be the witch around here?'

'Well, yes, but I'm your faithful wizard, you know that.'

I sigh. 'Fucking *feral horse*! If you must know, I'm having thoughts about my life.'

'What kind of thoughts?'

'They're not fully formed yet. Still marinating. Can I tell you when I know what's going on myself?'

'Yes, as long as you're okay?'

'I'm fine, mostly. And I'm over the moon for you, Milo. You've worked so hard for this.'

'I have, haven't I? Should we have a little phone party to celebrate?'

My heart lifts at the very thought of this. 'Like magic, I've got some tins of grapefruit G&T in the fridge. It's meant to be.'

'*Winner!*'

I run to the kitchen. Script be damned: I'm having a phone party with my best mate.

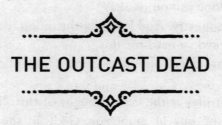

THE OUTCAST DEAD

I'm on the Tube and it's not packed for once, praise be. I had my chat with Charlie, who sounded like a very serious cockney geezer and was more grateful than I expected when I called. I now have an address on Union Street where his sister's boyfriend used to live. She was called Jill. The flats there are very expensive to rent now but were nowhere near as exclusive ten years ago. I've googled the place and it looks like a solid council block, with brick balconies running down the whole frontage. I like those little balconies because you can put plants and flowers out there and make it feel like you have some outdoor space, without having to do any gardening. I can't garden; if it's green, I kill it. Not on purpose. I've just got murder fingers when it comes to plants.

The boyfriend in question wasn't a junkie, as far as Charlie knows, simply a toker who said he was an artist and lived on benefits. The missing sister, Jill, who was clever and had recently got a good job, was happy to overlook his jobless status because she thought he was talented and, as she put it to Charlie, 'a total sex-god'. Charlie got very choked when he spoke of his sister; he obviously loved her a lot. I also have the address of the corner shop on the high street that caught Jill on CCTV; a corner shop that unfortunately doesn't exist in that form any more, as it's now an artisanal cheese shop.

Armed with the addresses and info I've gleaned, I get off at London Bridge, come out on Borough High Street and consider going into the Costa next door for a giant coffee. I decide to resist and have one on the way home instead, as I'll probably need the toilet within ten minutes of drinking it. I cross the road, walking left, past the shops and tourists. There are plenty of attractions south of the river, including the London Dungeon, plus there's Borough Market, so there are lots of people about.

Thinking of the London Dungeon reminds me of another attraction in the area that I visited a couple of years ago, and I shudder. The whole 'experience' involved me, Elsa and two of her workmates walking around these underground tunnels, emerging into gruesome rooms with blood-soaked tableaux peopled by 'zombies'. We went there on an afternoon for some reason and there were no other customers – just twenty minutes' worth of us trying to escape claustrophobic tunnels and creepy rooms inhabited by very bored actors caked in bloody make-up. They were obviously bursting to demonstrate their zombie skills, because they quickly became a terrifying mob, chasing us around the place, howling and growling; Elsa began to hyperventilate for real while her friends screamed the place down, and I got so frustrated by the whole thing that

I stopped in my tracks, turned and smacked a male zombie in the face, while bellowing, '*Leave us the fuck alone!*' I'm now banned from there for life, but I don't care. He was only knocked out for about three seconds, the snivelling baby, and I'm pretty sure he wasn't meant to get that close anyway.

I turn right onto Union Street and the shadows from the buildings make it chillier here than on the main road. Very quickly I'm in front of the block of flats that I saw on Google. The boyfriend's flat was on the first floor, three along. I can see that door from here. I stand still and slow my breath, see if I feel anything. Nothing. I walk back to Borough High Street towards the cheese shop. I take it slow and look at the image of the flame-haired young woman that Charlie texted me as I walk.

Feeling nothing but the swoosh of people walking far too close to me – *God, I hate that* – I reach the cheese deli, which smells bloody ripe, then I turn back, ambling to the front of the flats again. There's a lad sitting on the corner of Union Street with a blanket on his head and a ripped shellsuit on. He has a filthy face, but a friendly smile. London is full of these poor sods. I give him the one-pound coin I have in my purse (I never really carry cash because I'll spend it), before I'm standing opposite the flat door again. To my absolute disappointment, I still feel nothing at all.

Whoomph!

Out of the blue, I get the strongest pull to the bottom of Union Street, the other way from where I just walked. I 'protect' myself, imagining a warm light completely surrounding me, then allow whatever is calling to drag me to the bottom of the street and onto Redcross Way. A few steps and I'm looking at a sign by a gate: CROSS BONES GRAVEYARD. Bloody hell, I've never heard of this: what is it? There's a metal fence all the way down the front, with ribbons and plaques and dreamcatchers and all sorts of colourful commemorations tied over it. This place is amazing.

Inside, I see concrete and spaced-out flowerbeds and planters. It's tiny and there aren't any gravestones. *How can this be a graveyard?* As usual, no answer from Frank, but as I touch the metal fence next to the entrance it feels like I've been electrocuted. Energy, throbbing life and graceless death. Grief, the strongest grief. And so many people – so many, milling about, that I 'feel' the movement. There's a vibration that seems new; it's not like these spooks have been here for ages. It's like they just turned up and are running amok. Plus, the strangest of feelings: excitable kids. Loads and loads of little children. Running and playing. *Where the hell did they come from?*

I've never experienced anything this strong. It's so overwhelming that I let go of the fence, and read the plaque in front of me:

IN MEDIEVAL TIMES THIS WAS AN
UNCONSECRATED GRAVEYARD FOR PROSTITUTES
OR 'WINCHESTER GEESE'. BY THE EIGHTEENTH
CENTURY IT HAD BECOME A PAUPERS' BURIAL
GROUND, WHICH CLOSED IN 1853. HERE, LOCAL
PEOPLE HAVE CREATED A MEMORIAL SHRINE.
THE OUTCAST DEAD. R.I.P.

At the top of the plaque is a picture of a honking goose, neck outstretched. I look through the bars again, in case anyone is about, and right then I feel a hand on my arm. I turn and look down at the tiniest, oldest woman ever. She's wearing a blue linen coat and a matching linen bucket hat with a purple-and-yellow plastic pansy pinned to it. She has a string bag with oranges in it and pale, watery eyes. She looks like she knows everything that ever happened since time began, like my very, very old nanna, who was probably here before Moses. I am struck by an overwhelming desire to shout, 'Oh my *God*, how old are you?'

But before I can say anything, she nods towards the cemetery and says, 'It's open from twelve 'til three when there's a volunteer available.'

Her voice is like a tiny, fluttering wren. She smiles and has surprisingly good teeth for one so ancient. I love old people, me.

'Thank you.'

'Welcome.'

She shuffles off. As I watch her leave, I touch the metal railing again, but this time I can feel only the tiniest echo of what hit me before. A childish giggle and a lady weeping, then nothing.

I need to talk to Sheila about this. And I need coffee with cake *immediately*. I set off back to the Tube station, determined to google the shit out of Cross Bones Graveyard as soon as I'm home.

ORGANIC WINE AND A FRUITY VAPE

Sheila was so ill while I was filming that at first I'm worried that she's up and dressed. I expected to find my favourite psychic medium holding court from her High Priestess bed, with golden bowls of grapes and healing wine. But no, here she is at 6 p.m. sitting in her favourite chair, adorned in silky trousers and a long, thin sweater, French doors open, puffing away like Ivor the Engine. But not on a cigarette! No, Sheila now vapes. And despite the bags under her eyes, which show how ill and tired she's been, her skin looks much healthier.

I waft the fruity fug with my hand while I stare at my friend, who isn't even coughing.

'The antibiotics worked a treat, love. Those bloody knockout ones that mean you can't have a glass of wine or you'll collapse. That was a pain in the bum, but listen . . .'

She breathes deeply, and the wheeze is all but gone.

'Troy made me his soup and special stews for weeks. He was a total treasure. Got a bit loved up, though, so he's only allowed to visit once a week at the minute. He must get a girl his own age; going goo-goo-eyed over me is total non-sense. He needs to make some babies, or his mother will be after him.'

'Oh no, have you chucked him?'

Sheila twinkles at me. 'Who said anything actually happened between us?'

She's such a dark horse. She met her handsome Jamaican 'friend' when doing a tarot reading for him at the New Age shop where we used to work, and ultimately saved him from going to prison. Now he's become quite the fixture, it seems.

'Anyway, Tanz, come on, what happened today?'

She has furnished us both with a glass of lovely black-currant red wine, which she proudly announced is 'organic from Sainsbury's'. It shows how seriously she's taken this illness that she's replaced smoking with her puffety-puff machine and is drinking organic wine. I'm impressed. I watch as Sheila settles back in her chair, obviously ready for a long story. I take a deep breath and tell her about my unsuccessful attempt at 'feeling' Jill, Charlie's sister. Then about Cross Bones.

'Oh yes, the paupers' cemetery.'

'You know it?'

'Of course, the Winchester Geese!'

'Get you, smarty-pants. I've spent the afternoon studying the place and it's fascinating. Those prostitutes were pimped by the Bishop of Winchester, pimped by the *Church*, but were simply chucked into unconsecrated ground once they died. God had no room for those particular servants, did he?'

'Priests are very selective about who God would approve of.'

'Aren't they just? Thing is, though, it wasn't only the flippin' prostitutes. It went on to become the graveyard for paupers, which in Southwark over the ages was most of the population. There was so much poverty there, and the parish got a payout for everyone it buried because, of course, the families were too poor to pay for funerals themselves. They reckon, all told, there's fifteen thousand paupers and prostitutes buried in that tiny space – including loads of kids.'

When I think of those children I could cry. There seemed to be so many of them, running about or sitting in the dirt as tiny toddlers; filthy, undersized, but laughing. When I looked up the cemetery, I read that there's an area solely for children. Cholera, typhus, TB, malnourishment, measles . . . so many things that poor kids died of. It makes me feel sick. It also makes me want to go back there and try to talk to them, ask them what on earth they're doing there.

Sheila whistles. 'Fifteen thousand is a lot!'

'Will you go there with me, Sheils, when you feel up to it? I want to know why so many of the dead are hanging around.'

'Oh, I'd love to. I've not had a day trip on the Tube for ages. And I love it around London Bridge – we can go to Borough Market! Let's go this week.'

'Great. I didn't get there today, and I fancy some Polish sausage.'

She winks. 'I'll bet you do. Let's go and see what's going on with the Winchester Geese!'

I smile at my friend. There's no denying it: the colour is returning to those cheeks, but I definitely need to treat her to her favourite chocolates and cheese when we get to Borough Market. I'm determined to force some meat back on those bones. I need Sheila in my life for at least another hundred years.

JAZZ HANDS HAVE FALLEN OFF

I think I'm asleep. I usually know when I'm dreaming, but right now it's like I have a foot in two worlds. I can wonder to myself, *Am I asleep?* but I also know that there is a woman close by me and she's real. I can't see anything – it's dark in the way that it's dark when you squint your eyes shut – but I can hear the light clatter of a machine. It might be a sewing machine, but it's not an electric one. The voice is earthily melodic:

> '*I've found my bonny babe a nest On Slumber Tree,*
> *I'll rock you there to rosy rest, Asthore Machree!*
> *Oh, lulla lo! sing all the leaves On Slumber Tree,*
> *'Til everything that hurts or grieves Afar must flee.*
> *I've put my pretty child to float Away from me,*
> *Within the new moon's silver boat On Slumber Sea.*
> *And when your starry sail is o'er From Slumber Sea,*
> *My precious one, you'll step to shore On Mother's*
>   *Knee.'*

The machine stops and I can hear breathing. Then a voice.

'*Who's there?*'

Her accent is strange. London with a dash of Irish at the same time. She sounds scared.

'*Is it really you?*'

Before I can work out what the hell is going on, my phone rings and my eyes are springing open. I'm on the sofa, and Inka is snuggled on my lap. I must have fallen into a doze watching *Homes Under the Hammer*. That's the thing with red wine, no matter how much I sleep after drinking it, the next day I still feel snoozy. It's not even noon and I'm napping. Jesus! And, annoyingly, I've missed what that couple did with the two-up, two-down ramshackle mess they bought in Llandudno for nearly nothing. I love Wales, and it was giving me ideas.

It's Bill on the phone. I consider not answering, but I have to. I've been putting off giving him an answer about that play. Time to bite the bullet.

'Hello, Bill.'

'What's wrong with your voice? Have you got a cold?'

I don't want to tell him that I currently live a life of sleep, extra naps and kissing my cat's lovely soft forehead, with alcohol thrown in, so I lie.

'Just a bit of a sore throat. Rest and honey-and-lemon and I'll be fine.'

'Good stuff. Come on then, have you got an answer for *Truth Teller*? They start rehearsing on Monday and they're adamant their second choice is nowhere near as good as you. That's how much they love you.'

With a heavy heart, I concede to myself that I'm being lazy.

'Okay, tell them yes. I'll read it again later and get my head around the part.'

'Good lass. Looking forward to seeing you onstage again. I'm fucking sick of seeing the same faces in everything. I'll email all the times, dates and itinerary later. See ya!'

I sit up and Inka allows herself to be lifted and held against my chest. I think it's my chat with Elsa that's done this. Elsa, of all people, has started acknowledging what's right and good for her. A few years ago, you couldn't have prised her out of London for love or money. She was completely besotted with what she saw as the London lifestyle. She had so many instances of no money, bitchy people working alongside her on magazines shattering her confidence, thefts, muggings and, more recently, a depression-causing ghost in her home. She weathered it all. Now reality has hit even her and she's making practical decisions for an easier life.

I've been scared to admit it for ages, but I know that something about acting hasn't been working for me for quite a while. I think it has to do with needing to inhabit the heads of other people to escape my own. I've always over-thought and wobbled mentally, so escaping into a role meant I could immerse myself in someone else's life, be paid for it and get praise. Praise is something that used to be my lifeblood. Now, though, now I get to see into other people's heads and lives in a very different way, and suddenly it isn't all about me. I've tapped into the pain, suffering and loves of those who are now departed, and all at once showing off seems the most embarrassing of occupations.

I lay my chin on Inka's purring head as I tentatively check my options. I don't see what else I can do. Shop wages and other badly paid jobs will not cover my ridiculous rent. I've tried them all. Plus I haven't got the patience for a full-time job in anything. People who do 'proper' jobs deserve a knighthood and three thousand medals each. I must take acting jobs when they come, because they sometimes pay very well. No other job that I'm capable of can top up the bank balance in the same way. But it's precarious, and it doesn't change the fact that my jazz hands seem to have fallen off. I simply can't drum up the enthusiasm for crappy characters, or the patience for waiting and waiting for acting work that is random, infrequent and, these days, seldom satisfying. On top of that, I've been doing this for ages. I always play younger, I'm older than I look, and it stands to reason that I'm feeling the pull towards a life less shallow. I want what I do to *mean* something. When did that happen?

'*Why do you think I showed up when I did?*'

'Oh, hello, Frank. To be honest, you only show up when you bloody well please, so how would I know?'

'*You don't need me all the time. In fact, I'm sending another helper to you for a bit. They might come in handy.*'

'Oh?'

'*Yep, no worries, you're getting the hang of things, but there's stuff that is beyond even Sheila now. That's why you're having a paddy at the minute. That and you're a right drama queen.*'

'Shut up!'

'Change is coming, it's good.'

'Frank, why do I keep thinking I'm living the wrong life?'

'You're adjusting. I don't say this very often and I don't expect it all the time, but . . . I'm proud of you. What you're doing is important. You're very brave.'

Oh God, that nearly has me blubbing. I don't think nice thoughts about me. To be honest, I don't think about myself at all in a positive way. I'm such a fucking ramshackle mess half the time; what's to think about, apart from negative brain-shit and trying not to get fat because, as an actress, that's the biggest sin? A sin I don't agree with at all, I hasten to add, because I love food. I think that the telly and films and stage should be crammed with every shape and size and colour and accent and quirk. But that's not my call, unfortunately.

'I don't know how to be a normal person, Frank, and I don't know what my function is.'

'Your function? You are not a HOOVER. Just follow your instincts to the letter. That's it. Listen and act accordingly. You're my total favourite.'

I feel Frank leave. A sense of helplessness engulfs me. I've been sitting here chatting with a dead person in my head. That's who I am now – I have mates who don't have bodies. Anyone I talk to about this, apart from Sheila and Gladys back at home, will make a judgement on it. Why would I even consider trying to be 'normal'?

Luckily there's an unopened packet of fig rolls in the kitchen to stop me from going into absolute despair; you can't drink coffee, eat fig rolls and be depressed – that's a natural law. I gently place Inka back on the sofa and go to put the kettle on. A full cafetière, fig rolls and my new play: that's the afternoon sorted. I was thinking of going for a run, but sod that.

GHOST PARTY

It was threatening rain when Sheila and I got on the Tube, but when we emerge onto Borough High Street from the yawning tunnels – Sheila in all of her rings and a long green paisley skirt, me in my favourite multicoloured Thai trousers – the sun has broken out. People have unwrapped scarves, unbuttoned heavy coats and are generally looking a little less miserable than people in London usually look. The shell suit lad is there again on the corner of Union Street. He always seems to have a dirty pink fleece blanket draped over his head, and his shell suit is extremely ripped at the knee. He's sitting on cardboard and is removing a pulled-apart bin bag that he'd been using as a makeshift rain shelter. A young lass with lank, long hair and a white Staffordshire Bull Terrier with the softest eyes is walking away from him, cackling, clutching a tin of lager. Sheila hands him some change and he grins up at us, a broad Yorkshire accent emerging as he says, 'All the thanks from blanket land!'

I lead the way to the graveyard, careful not to walk too

fast as I'm still not totally convinced Sheila isn't going to relapse. She's oblivious, happily sucking away on her vape, sending plumes of fruity, minty steam into the air. I checked online and, unless I'm much mistaken, we'll be able to go into Cross Bones Graveyard today. I point out the flat on Union Street as we walk and Sheila stops and looks up at the door; her face becomes thoughtful as she 'goes within', then she takes another drag on her vape and shakes her head.

'Can't feel a thing, love. Whatever happened to Jill, if anything did, it didn't happen here. I mean, it might have happened in that flat, but it feels completely dead – excuse the pun – energy-wise. Nothing coming from the windows or door.'

'That's a relief. I thought my powers were failing me.'

'Don't be daft. I get the feeling that the brother might be barking up the wrong tree with the boyfriend. I can't feel a bloody thing, and usually there'd be some vestige of feeling if a murder had happened.'

'I think you're right. Charlie said the boyfriend's story was that Jill had told him she wanted to marry him, and he'd told her he wasn't the marrying type; he said it wasn't an argument as the boyfriend had told Jill before that he never wanted to get married. They'd had a bottle of wine by then and were going to have some food, but she got upset with him and told him he needed to grow up. Apparently, they hardly raised their voices. Neighbours corroborated this. Jill left, called into the shop for a couple of bottles of wine and that's the last anybody saw of her.

There were a couple of supposed sightings, but nothing they could prove. She simply vanished.'

Sheila wrinkles her nose.

'Why women get so het up about marrying blokes is well beyond me, Tanz. It's like hitching yourself to a wobbly cart with broken wheels. Nothing but a heavy burden, practically from the start.'

'All right, "Sheila's Marriage Counselling". I'm not sure I would shag a wobbly cart. That aside, it's a weird little story, and it would be so nice to be able to help Charlie. He was so sweet and accepting when I told him I hadn't felt anything. I want to solve it.'

'Ask your guides. If it's meant to be solved, it will be. Meantime, come on, I'm itching to see Cross Bones Graveyard.'

I lead on until we reach the gate and the ranks of coloured ribbons and paraphernalia on the railings. I can't believe how strong the energy is. I must get inside. Sheila gives one of her little whistles.

'Bloody hell, Tanz, it's like Grand Central Station in there. Graveyards aren't usually rammed with the energy of this many souls – they've usually moved on. What's going on?'

'Told you.'

She closes her eyes for a moment.

'This is very strange. This doesn't feel like layers of ghosts getting older and older as time stretches back. This feels like they all turned up at once, like a spooked-up street party.'

'See! Let's get in there.'

I THINK I JUST DIED

A lovely lady called Louisa greets us as we come through the gate, and we get a wave from a lady at the other end who's tending a bush near the white wall at the back. Louisa has a jaunty scarf wrapped round her head and looks all gorgeous and Mediterranean. The other lady is called Heather, apparently, and is in dark-green gardening clothes and wellies. There are such lovely flowerbeds and banks of plants, and different 'areas' separated by concreted ground. It can't take away from the fact that this place is tiny, though. I cannot comprehend the idea of fifteen thousand bodies being buried here. Sheila and I look around, with Louisa telling us the story of the bodies that were dug up when Transport for London was extending the Jubilee Line. When we reach the children's bit, with its statues and beautiful greenery, it becomes hard to concentrate. I cannot believe the energy that hits me in the solar plexus and chest. I glance at Sheila, who is also looking a little breathless.

'Oh, ladies. Many people get overwhelmed at this part

of the graveyard. All those poor children; the Mizuko Jizō statues are here to help people reflect on the loss of their babies and young ones. They're beautiful, aren't they?'

'They really are, Louisa, love. The whole thing is gorgeous. Quite overwhelming. I wondered if we could sit down on the bench over there for a bit? Take it all in?'

'Oh, of course. You are so welcome – that's what it's there for. It's nice to have you ladies here; you care, I can tell.'

Sheila nods. 'The way you look after this place, love. You're diamonds.'

She's looking a bit tearful. We sit and I take her hand.

'Are you okay, Sheils?'

'Yes. Just remembering something I try to forget.'

I strongly feel this is not the time to probe further. My poor friend; why is life so hurtful to people? I don't take my hand away but draw in a deep breath and slowly take in the whole place.

'I can really sense something. It's like this place called me here, Sheila.'

'Well, with me here, you'll tune in even more. Why don't you close your eyes and see what comes?'

She holds my hand more tightly and I do as I'm told. I close my eyes and ask whatever guide is with me (Frank said he was sending someone new, so I keep my options open) to help me tune in. I feel everything growing still and absolutely quiet, and then open my eyes inwardly and look around.

It's still day. Well, I think it's day, but the sky is a strange yellow colour I've never seen before and it's drizzling miserably. I draw in a breath, but it's shallow and it hurts my chest. My hands, *flippin' heck*, they've got veins like ropes and there are liver spots. They're an old man's hands and I'm holding a shovel; it's heavy and I'm digging into mud that's becoming slimy. Then the stench hits me: Jesus, it stinks. It's fetid. I look around to see where the smell might be coming from as my old man's hands push the shovel hard into the soft ground, and I see a muddy turnip plop out right next to my feet. There are a few of these turnips and . . . *what's that?* Weird lumps of meat. Then I notice the meat has fingers and the turnips are made of bone – they're skulls, skulls lying about the place, with flesh and maggots everywhere.

Before I can scream, I'm in a little dark room. There's a tiny open fire, which is burning low with no heat. I can make out a window. There's a rag hanging in front of it and there's very little light. Again, it reeks. This time it's urine, and something worse. There's a metal cup of some sort grasped in my veiny hand, with watery-looking tea in it. I hear coughing, distant persistent coughing, and I see the cup fall from my hand. The cup hits the sawdust on the floor with a far-off thunk. The coughing is becoming a wheeze. Then there's the sound of a woman screaming, desperate cries: *'You pulled him back out – my boy, my lovely boy, out of the ground . . . Why would you? Why?'*

Then the room darkens further and suddenly the floor whooshes towards me, and I feel a thud, then open my eyes.

Sheila is holding my hand and we're still sitting on the bench overlooking the concreted ground and a little garden plot. The sun is trying really hard to peek out from behind the clouds. It's so nice to escape the stink and breathe fresh air again.

'You all right, love?'

'Fucking hell, Sheila. I think I just died.'

'You what?'

'I was inside someone when they died. It all went black, I didn't see what came next, but—'

I let go of her hand and she takes out her vape.

'I was here still, I think, but when it was soil and earth. I was a gravedigger. It was raining and I was digging bodies back up. They weren't even properly rotted away yet. It stank. There were skulls and clumps of half-rotted flesh with bones in them.'

'Bloody hell!'

'I know. And I could see my hands; they looked ancient. Not that I think people round here lived 'til they were ancient in the old days, but they were old hands, and there was a weariness when I looked at them. A weariness of the heart. He'd not had an easy life, but also he was scared, as well as suffering from tiredness and a pain in the chest. Then I was somewhere else – his home, I reckon. Poor sod. It was a little hovel of a place, which stank as well. I don't think his hygiene was great, but it smelled of open drains and rotting food in there. Really awful. And he was cold. It was so cold, despite him lighting a tiny fire. Then he was coughing. I think he had a chest infection or something; that hacking noise you get from deep, deep within. Anyway, I was him, and suddenly the coughing and breathing stopped and I hit the floor; it was soft, then he was gone. I got a feeling this was the nineteenth century; I need to look up how people lived in those days, and why it stank of shit!'

'In the poorer boroughs they had open sewers in the streets until much more recently than you might think. We need to look up Southwark. I know there were slums all around here. Why was he digging bodies up?'

'From what I've read, it was to make way for the new ones. Southwark parish wanted the money for the new burials.'

'Charming.'

'I know. I've got more reading to do. Plus, just to say, Sheila, you would not have appreciated what passed for a cup of tea then.'

She laughs, then stares somewhere around my knees.

'Tanz?'

'Yes?'

'There's a toddler in front of you, cuddling into your leg.'

As soon as she says it, I can feel a weight against my left leg, but I can't see anything.

'How are they so powerful? I can feel them everywhere. Why are they here?'

'I don't know. This is like no other graveyard I've visited before. Dead people don't usually haunt where they're buried. There's something going on here, but I don't know what it is. It's a one-off. Quite exciting really.'

I close my eyes and visualize the child against my leg. Suddenly I can see this tiny girl. I only know she's a girl because she's clutching a stained cloth dolly and she has sandy-coloured curls. But she's filthy, with a snotty nose, gigantic dark eyes and what looks like a ripped-up sheet for clothes. She's teensy and adorable. She smiles gappily at me, and I notice she has red marks all over her. I think she must have died of measles. Poor thing.

When I open my eyes again, Sheila is looking at me.

'Polish sausage?'

'I should cocoa.'

We both stand.

SCOUSE SQUEALS

Borough Market is stuffed with lovely trinkets, fresh produce and street food and sprawls across several roads. We call at a cheese stall, where a wonderful French lass serves me a gorgeous slab of truffle Brie, which I immediately present to Sheila as a gift. (I also get a tiny slice for myself. I mean, who the fuck doesn't love truffle Brie?) I then buy my huge smoked sausage as planned, with extra onions, and Sheila has some pad thai, which smells flippin' delicious. We eat sitting on a wall by the water, overlooking a pub that has nice outside tables, but which I really need to avoid because alcohol is a bit too enmeshed in my life right now. We are only a few feet away from the *Golden Hinde*, the beautiful replica of Sir Francis Drake's galleon, which is moored on Bankside, by the Clink.

The Clink Prison Museum is one of my favourite places in London, which is why I'm so shocked that I didn't know about Cross Bones, when it's so close. The Clink dates back to 1144, and the museum is built on the original site. It's gruesome and informative, with lots of terrifying examples of how prisoners were treated in the olden times. I love to go there and look at the brutal torture devices, which I think says a bit too much about me and my dark brain. But my favourite bit is where they've got an example of the old walls of the tenement streets in London, showing how close together buildings were in those days; this explains not only the fire hazard, but why it was dangerous to move around certain boroughs at night. There was hardly room for two people to pass through some of those little streets; it was no place for anyone who was claustrophobic or wanted to hang on to their purse. Walking between those close walls literally makes me hold my breath – and that's in a museum. What the hell must it really have been like? As I eat, I start reading to Sheila from Google.

'"Close to the Clink stand the ruins of Winchester Palace. They're very tall, with a huge window still intact. Just looking up at the walls gives you an idea of how enormous the palace was. How different the lives of the rich and the poor . . . The Clink was one of two prisons in the grounds. One was for women and one for men. Which means the Bishop of Winchester (the title got passed down) owned the palace, the prison and offered some protection to the prostitutes he 'owned'."'

Sheila rolls her eyes.

'Protection, my foot. Church or not, it was simply men using women, as usual.'

I take another bite of juicy meat and onions and scan the rest of the article.

'Apparently this part of London was filled with theatres, bear-pits, taverns and brothels, or "stews", for five hundred bloody years. And the ladies from the "stews" were tossed into the Cross Bones Graveyard after they died, once it opened in 1598 as the "Single Woman's churchyard". Sheila, I don't mean to be disrespectful, but bishops seem to have been absolute bastards since Christianity started.'

'Yup.'

'From what I'm reading, those women usually died young, doing the job that the bishop wanted them to do. Priests were smuggling toffs to London Bridge via boat "the back way" so that no one found them out. Then they were chucking the women who did that work into a shitty little cemetery when they'd clapped out.'

'I told you. Men are nothing but trouble. Churchmen, non-churchmen – we're expendable. Bloody keep away from them.'

I can't help laughing.

'Sheila, there are some nice men.'

'I know. But it takes ages to suss them; best just keep away. Or at least never live with any.'

She's hilarious. And with my past record of choosing very badly, she may have a point. She stabs at a last noodle with a peanut on top of it and looks at me levelly.

'I'll tell you something I've learned, and I really mean it. When you're younger, great sex with a brooding or charismatic man is such a high. You think you want to marry them, and you'll love each other for ever. But then you start liking yourself and not needing to prove a damn thing, and suddenly "brooding" means moody and boring; "charismatic" usually means full of ego and always with an eye on the ladies. And sex . . . well, unless they're considerate and loving towards you, it's simply bloody gymnastics. Nothing you couldn't achieve yourself with a good toy.'

There are two older women sitting a few feet away, eating what seem to be Mexican wraps. The oldest-looking of the two has a jolly, round face and very red cheeks and she turns as Sheila finishes. She grins, raises a thumb and says in a loud Liverpool accent, 'If someone had told me that when I was younger, I'd have bought a rampant rabbit and told the bastard I married to do one! Sorry to earwig, but that's one of the best things I've ever heard!'

Sheila winks.

'Nothing like bitter experience to teach you what you need to know years after it's too late!'

The lady laughs and her friend joins in.

'Well, he's gone now and me and my mate Lainey here, we can come down to London, drink what we want, eat what we want and see as many musicals as we want. The kids are grown, that bastard's launched himself on someone else and I'm free.'

Lainey gives a slightly apologetic shrug. 'I'm still with mine; he's quite nice really.'

'Yeah, she got a good one, so they do exist. I think there are about three in the world, and Lainey found one of them.'

The friends laugh together, and I notice that with their lunch they're each drinking a can of vodka and cranberry. Sheila suddenly looks hard at the first lady who spoke to us.

'What's your name, love?'

'Oh, I'm Dawn. Nice to meet you.'

'I'm Sheila, Dawn, and I'm afraid you're in trouble here. There's a bloke lives near you, plays darts with another member of your family. Your brother maybe? He's liked you for ages, and he asked you out and you said no. He's a good one.'

Lainey squeals, and Dawn goes even redder than she already was.

'Oh my God, you mean Dev? I've known him since school. He's always said he fancied me, but he's . . . too nice. A bit quiet.'

'Let me tell you, Dawn, you won't think that after a night in the sheets with him.'

Two Scouse voices squeal with laughter in unison at this. Sheila's face becomes more serious.

'Also, Dawn, you've had a pain in your side. Go to the doctor. It's nothing serious yet. Get it checked out and you'll be fine. Okay?'

'Bloody hell, how did you know that? Are you a witch? Have we met a witch in London?'

We stand to leave and Sheila twinkles at them.

'You've met two witches in London.'

We hear more Scouse squeals as we make our retreat.

Funny old day.

BEAUTIFUL MEG AND
THE SOFT-VOICED LASS

I'm walking through close-together streets, almost like they have in the Clink, but with a little more passing room. There are threadbare clothes strung between the windows, the brickwork is filthy and there are a lot of children. There are kids in various stages of undress all over the place. They're mostly shoeless and are playing happily in the mud, like it's normal.

The stench!

Cesspit. I smelled a cesspit in the countryside next to my campsite when I was little. You never forget that whiff. It's really strong here. Mixed with horse shit, which seems to be everywhere. The street looks muddy, but it isn't mud; it's shite and, by the smell of the liquid turning it into mud, the place is literally running with urine. I hear horses' hooves up ahead and realize that there must be a lot of horses relieving themselves around here. The ammonia is so strong it stings my eyes. There's soot on all the walls, it appears, and the air is heavy with the fog of burning oil. I can feel the smoke lining my lungs. I rub my finger along the bricks as I walk, and it comes away pitch-black.

My hands are small and white, though they are bright red at the knuckles below the nails. I've read about this. Chilblains. Maidservants in the old days used to get chilblains. I'm carrying a pail with dirty-looking water in it. I have a grey shawl made of what seems to be rough linen and I'm in a hurry for something, though I don't know what. I reach a splintered front door and walk through and up three flights of stairs. The stairs are rickety and weak, the staircase so narrow and with so little natural light that it's a wonder people don't break their necks on it all the time.

I enter a room. A candle is burning low by a cot bed. A man lies on the bed. He doesn't look old, but he's shirtless and his chest is covered in a rash. He has a cracked basin by the bed, into which he's vomited. I can smell it. His hair is longish, and he has a thick moustache. I get a snatch – a memory of him – upright, smiling, pipe in his mouth. He's a good-looking fella when he's not ill. He is loved. But right now, he is suffering badly. From the darkened corner I hear a squeak and realize that the ill-shaped lump over there is a basket with a rag over it. There's a baby in it. The man on the bed stirs and looks right at me. A wave of protectiveness comes over me as I approach him, sit by his side and dip a cloth in the water, lovingly wiping his brow and face. His hand reaches out and takes mine.

'What's wrong with him?' I ask this with my mind, not expecting an answer. But a gentle female voice replies.

'*Typhus. You didn't always die from it, but he has weak lungs already from the factories.*'

'Oh no. Will he pull through?'

'No. First him; then the baby dies from the damp.'

'Fucksake! What can I do?'

'Nothing. Show love. Remember them. That's it.'

I reach out the hand that isn't mine and cup the man's face. I send every bit of love I have in me to him, through the eyes of this woman I don't even know. He smiles weakly back. Speaks. I hear him like he's far away.

'My beautiful Meg.'

Irish. Again Irish. Like Pat, from my short-lived love affair. And like the woman I heard at the sewing machine in my dream two nights ago. I want to do the same for the baby – go to it and give it love – but I can feel myself being pulled away, detaching from the scene.

Unwillingly I suddenly find myself awake in my room, light breaking through the blinds, cat on the mattress beside my pillow. I check the time. In two hours I set off for day one of my 'new job'. It takes a little while to shake the vision I just had. How did anyone find any happiness in those days if they were poor? I think of myself as poor, when I'm skint. But I'm not dying of horrible, preventable diseases or living on mouldy little cups of shitty tea. Plus, I have a bathroom. The sanitary arrangements in the old days were an OCD person's nightmare. I try to push my mind back towards today's job.

I've worked on the character as best I can, but she really is a total pain in the arse. The writer seems to have attempted to create a 'strong woman' who takes no shit, but comes off as try-hard, worthy and the most horribly politically correct weirdo. No sense of humour at all. And the characters around her speak like cardboard-cutout people. My character is the lead later; she's not in the play at first, and I'm hoping I might be able to inject some cheeky irony, to make the audience think we're in on some kind of secret together. You never know, the writer might be amenable to slight amendments. But the thing is, in real life I take no shit, and I'm nothing like this stiff automaton that the writer came up with. It's not easy being honest and people don't always like it. That's what being a take-no-shit woman is; you wind up pissing other people off. The writer should have based it on me.

Anyway I need coffee now, and my mind keeps going back to whatever the hell I just saw in my 'dream'. This is what happens when you study the conditions in Southwark in the olden days – it starts bloody haunting you. Also, who did that voice belong to? It certainly wasn't Frank, it was a youngish-sounding woman.

'Hello, soft-voiced lass, are you there?'

No reply.

Well, it was worth a go, wasn't it? Maybe it was simply a dream, like that weird one the other night with the woman in the dark. I have no idea what the hell that was all about, either. As long as I don't start dreaming about that horrible bastard in Newcastle again, I'll be all right. I moved him on, so it should be fine, but I still get a prickle of fear mixed with outrage every time I think of him 'possessing' Milo and scaring the bloody life out of us both. Ghosts can be total shits. This new lot haven't been shits yet, but they do make me feel sad and totally confused.

What do they want?

LEATHER BLOUSON JACKET

Christ, I'm aware that I'm a drama queen, but the trip to Angel from Finsbury Park is a million times more troublesome than it should be. Traffic jams on the bus ride, Tube stuck in a tunnel, passengers rammed in and angry. By the time I spill out of the station I'm already frazzled and considering the journey a bad omen. I've only got minutes to spare, so I don't even have time to grab a rehearsal cappuccino as I cross the road and enter the Old Red Lion.

I love this place. It's had a theatre since 1979, but the pub itself is very, very old and the building is fab. Highwaymen and footpads used to drink here: how cool is that? (Unless you were robbed by one of them; not so cool then, I suppose.) Today I smile and wave at who I presume to be the new theatre manager who's standing by the bar. He's called Tom. I had an email from him, briefly outlining the rules of the building and so on, but I haven't met him yet. Emails have little photographs up in the corner, though, and that's him as he has a magnificent ginger beard.

'Hey, Tanz, good luck!'

'Thanks, Tom, catch up later?'

I run straight up the stairs to the theatre space, which I know well. I've already told myself to sort my head out and behave like a professional. Last time I worked here I was twenty-four and I was in a comedy called *Toot Toot* with three people who are now much more famous than I am. We had a blast, and at the time I wanted to find a good play, raise the money and direct it myself. I had all these ideas. The beauty of this place is that the productions self-finance, then the box office splits the door takings, so you have a theatre where you can put on your own plays and pay yourself back from the ticket sales. The problem with that being, of course, that if you don't advertise the show properly as director/producer, you could lose a few grand. When I was last here, the play was a hit and no one lost a dime. After my initial enthusiasm, I wasn't so sure I could emulate that, so I lost confidence and didn't do it after all.

Today, as I walk through the top door straight into the muted theatre lights, I see a small bunch of actors sitting in the flip-up stall seats. Onstage on a plastic chair is the man who must be the director, in a leather blouson jacket, his doughy face prickled with designer stubble. Standing beside him is a lass dressed in a denim skirt, cowboy boots and a draped shirt that needs one more button doing up, in my opinion. She's about thirty, carrying a ring binder and leaning against the side of his chair. I don't even have to speak to them to know they're fucking. She's establishing ownership with her body language, and he's holding court:

the man who has it all. Yes, I am that judgemental. And I'll bet I'm totally right about them.

As I enter, the director stands.

'Tanz! Hello, I'm Brett. Thank you for agreeing to play the part of Perdita. This is Maeve, the writer.'

Maeve thrusts out her hand and for a second I think she wants me to kiss it.

'Hello, Maeve.'

I shake her fingers. She has straight, shiny dark hair, which she flicks coltishly over one shoulder and smiles broadly. She has shiny white teeth, but her eyes don't smile with her mouth. It's weird how someone can be beautiful on paper, but actually have a bland face at the same time. Brett approaches and puts his arm around me, like we're old friends (he smells very strongly of a lemony cologne and Lynx; it clashes a bit). He then introduces me to the people sitting in the 'audience'. There are two very young actors, a girl with a long blonde bob and a boy with a foppish fringe, who are both around eighteen or nineteen. Claire and Peter. They seem sweet and not overly nervous, and I like both on sight. But my favourite is the older bloke in the next row back. He's got a big face, a bulbous nose, slightly protruding eyes, a mouth that twitches at one side and a mop of white-grey hair with a bald patch and a combover.

'I'm Gerald.'

He has a proper old-school actor's voice and rounds his vowels hugely. I have seen him in stuff over the years – small but very enjoyable character parts onscreen – and I like his work immensely. I walk round and sit by him.

'Hello, Gerald, I've seen you in loads; you're a genius.'

He seems delighted that I've gravitated straight to the seat next to him. He whispers, 'Thank you, my dear.'

Brett nods and claps his hands together.

'Right, my dudes, now I've got my team together, let's have a chat about work. I have some great ideas about getting to grips with our characters, and I think you'll really enjoy them. I also think Maeve here has written quite a special play, and as it's one act and only an hour long, we can really explore it for the next fortnight. Would you like to add anything, Maeve, before we do our first read-through?'

She smiles again and opens her folder and, as she does so, Gerald speaks expertly to me from the corner of his mouth.

'Looks like it's not just the play he's been exploring.'

Oh God, it's so hard not to burst out laughing. I'm obviously not the only one to notice the sex hormones leaking out all over the place. I press my knee against his in acknowledgement.

Maeve clears her throat. She has a posh London accent and a piercing voice.

'So, I wrote this play about my young life. And how I became a strong and actualized woman. Everyone but Tanz plays several parts. Gerald's main part, as you know, is the God of Judgement. Well, he gets schooled, doesn't he? Tanz is my older self – no offence – the woman I will grow to be. Among other characters, Claire is more my age now—' I can't believe she said that; she's fucking ten years older than Claire, if she's a day '—and, Peter, you get to play all the men who oppressed me when I was younger. We'll need to get you a false beard for a couple of them.'

Gerald snorts. He takes out a tissue and pretends to blow his nose. Maeve looks at him and then, satisfied it was medical and not disparaging, she nods meaningfully at us actors.

'Now, as you know, we writers all have a special rhythm. Writing is music, so I would ask you to learn my lines as closely as possible. I want them to flow exactly as I wrote them, so please, no approximations – get them right.'

Fuck! So I can't change anything then? I'm pretty gutted by this, but hey, I'm here now, what can I do? Brett gives a nod to Maeve, who stops herself from actually taking a bow, then looks at us and claps twice.

'Right. We're going to start with a vocal warm-up before the read-through . . . so if you all want to come and join me on the stage.'

Claire and Peter are straight up there. I suppress a groan. Gerald looks at me and mouths, 'Oh, for fuck's sake.'

We both slowly join the others on the stage. Maeve sits in the front row, obviously not up for vocal acrobatics. Brett nods sagely.

'Please, everyone, hold hands and form a circle. I'll join you when I've pressed play. I have some music here; it's a bit different from the usual stuffy "acting" shit, yeah? Instead of that rubbish, let's make tonal noises to the music, bring out your inner truth, your inner beast. Whatever works for you, go for it – just do it from your gut, then you'll be ready.'

Brett presses play on a plastic boombox standing on a

table behind him, then joins the circle. Almost immediately a drum and bass track begins. I don't know what to do. Brett starts skipping from one foot to the other. Claire and Peter fall into step. Gerald, who is quite a large man, is in no way capable of jumping from one foot to the other that fast and begins to shake his hips. It's one of the funniest things I've ever seen. I begin to nod my head in time with his hip-shakes, and he looks at me like he wants to kill someone. Again, I have a huge urge to collapse into belly-laughs. Instead, I bite my lip, and Brett starts to make panting noises in time with the music. Peter goes on the second beat each time, saying, 'Da-da-da' and Claire says, 'Ooh-ooh-ooh' along with Peter. All I can think about is how Brett, if he continues to pant that quickly, will hyperventilate and faint.

I snatch a glance at Gerald, who is living a completely different life in his eyes. His face is serious, but his eyes tell me to follow his lead. Suddenly he lets out a caveman yowl. On every fourth beat he does it. I jump in and let out an almost sexual yelp on every third beat. I keep my face as serious as I can. Brett looks like he might orgasm. He suddenly lets out a primal howl, beckoning that we all join in, then turns off the stereo and whoops.

'All right!'

Maeve gives us a polite round of applause. I glance at Gerald, who is staring at his feet. Fuck me, how are we going to survive this rehearsal period? As I think this, suddenly Frank's voice appears in my head.

'*Your mam and dad would be so proud to see this.*'

'SOD OFF, YOU.'

NOBODY LIKES STUPID PEOPLE
TELLING THEM WHAT TO DO

We have a drink in the bar afterwards. Of course we do – it's been quite the day. The younger ones have a quick soft drink and then exit, probably to learn their lines and be diligent. They're both really nice. Claire has a great face and seems very innocent and kind (acting will knock that out of her soon enough), and Peter is gay as far as I can tell, talented and hungry for work. He's also very handsome, with a deep voice for someone so young, so I reckon he's going to go far.

Maeve and Brett stay upstairs to 'discuss' the play. I see one of the bar girls, a canny lass with fuchsia hair, go up with a bottle of red and two glasses, so that'll be them for the time being. Brett has one of those faces that men get when they're very slim but drink a lot, and like a line of coke or six. Their face gets this puffy look, even though they're not fat. He probably thinks he's hiding it with the stubble, but he isn't. I can spot it a mile off.

Gerald is drinking a pint with a whisky chaser, and I'm gulping back the biggest glass of Sauvignon Blanc they could give me. Once it's only the two of us, Gerald looks at me and wrinkles his big nose.

'Brett and Maeve.'

'What about them?'

'Pair of cunts.'

Oh goodness. A whole day of despair mixed with suppressed hysteria rises to the surface and I lose it. The laughter comes from the middle of my soul. And once I go, Gerald goes. What a circus of a day. After our 'vocal warm-up', the read-through went off predictably enough. Pretentious and self-indulgent was made flesh. But if that was pretentious, then Maeve's character breakdowns afterwards bordered on public masturbation and took up the rest of rehearsal time.

Gerald downs his whisky in one, then takes a swallow of his pint.

'Tanz, I don't think he's directed anything before. Not even traffic. The lad's a moron. As for her . . .' He sighs.

'She's not very bright, Gerald. I try not to judge, but I don't like thick people telling me what to do.'

'Nobody likes stupid people telling them what to do. Why are we here, Tanz? By the way, what sort of a name is Tanz?'

'It's short for Tania. No one calls me that, upon pain of death.'

'Can I? I like Tania.' He pronounces it 'Tarnia'. It sounds pretty awesome when he says it, with his received-pronunciation voice and big vowels.

'I can't believe I'm saying this, but yes, you can call me that. Just while we're rehearsing this fucking mess.'

'Why did you take this job, Tarnia?'

'Because my agent says I need to up my theatre profile. I'm not sure I want to up my bloody profile, though. What about you?'

'My wife is sick of the sight of me. I mostly do voice-overs these days. Adds nicely to the nest egg but doesn't take much time. Thought it might be fun to do a play, get out from under her feet and remember what it's like to be in a company.'

'I thought you were gay, Gerald. You're far too funny to be straight.'

'Darling, I'm an actor. I'm extremely sexually flexible.'

I laugh. 'What are we going to do?'

'Fuck knows, Tarnia – we're trapped.'

'Should we have another drink?'

'Yes, we fucking should.'

Thank *Christ* for Gerald.

When I've got us our next round, Gerald fixes me with an amused glare.

'You have done very well on television. My nosy wife looked you up on t'interweb. I think they brought you in to sell tickets, as well as be glorious. How are you going to make your character not shit, Tarnia? I have no hope, but maybe you can save yourself.'

'We haven't got a chance if we can't change a syllable. I think the question is how can we get through these rehearsals in one piece? It's only performed for a week, so we can limp through that. In the meantime, we need to be there for each other. And for the young ones, when they suddenly realize they're working on a piece of shit.'

'I think concentrating on our end-of-the-day drink will help a lot.'

'I think you're right. Let's toast to that, lad!'

As we're clinking glasses, our director and writer emerge from upstairs. Maeve's hair isn't as perfect as it was, and Brett's looking rather flushed. He grins when he sees us toasting each other.

'Celebrating a successful first day, I see. Well, I have to say, well done both of you; a bit of work and I think you're going to do yourselves – and Maeve's script – proud.'

She smiles that flat big-toothed smile, then launches her high-pitched voice. 'Yeah, rub the rough edges off you all and we're going to have some great performances.'

Her voice is so sharp I'm surprised a couple of pint glasses at the bar don't explode. She strokes Brett's arm and hoicks up her expensive powder-blue satchel containing the ring binder and fuck knows what else.

'Well, we'd better be going. Busy day tomorrow, making magic. See you both at ten sharp.'

I don't like how Maeve says that – pointedly. I wasn't late today, I was two minutes early, and the traffic and Tube had been shit.

As they exit, Gerald necks his latest Scotch.

'She's got the makings of a mini-Mussolini, that one. Mark my words, she'll be trying to take over within two days. Brett won't like it; he thinks he's the boss. Get ready for fireworks.'

'Really? It's almost worth not walking off the job just to see what the hell she does.'

'Don't you dare! You're not leaving me to live in this purgatory on my own.'

'How is it, Gerald, that the people with talent – the writers, the directors, the actors, the singers – sort of get left at the bottom? That the bastards and the incompetents seem to get the good chances and merrily fuck them up, while everyone praises them, and the rest of us do our best with shit and never really get noticed?'

'Oh, I think we all must give up on the idea of being noticed and simply milk every second of fun we can out of something that's sometimes thankless. I mean, come on, Tarnia, it can be quite ridiculous doing this; today was double awful with "fuck it" topping. But it's still not as bad or boring as being a temp in an office, is it? And I think a lot of actresses would be rather cross, hearing you class yourself as being left at the bottom. You've had quite an expansive number of bites at the cherry, have you not?'

'I have. In the past. And I'm very glad to meet you, Gerald. You're one of the old guard of good actors. I'm honoured.'

He sinks more of his pint.

'Why, thank you, my dear. Now, no more talk of leaving me all alone in hell with two good-looking children for company!'

The truth is, I've signed the contract. I can't walk without a lot of trouble. My only choice is to drink my way through this, with my new mate. Performing in this shitfest is going to be horrendous, but at least we have each other.

Next time, though, I'll listen to my instincts.

SHE WASN'T A GHOST

When I get home, there's a card waiting on the mat. The light bulb in my hallway is flickering; it's been doing that for a week, and I've been too lazy to sort it. I don't even have to buy a new bulb, as I have some in the kitchen. I'll do it tonight. I open the card straight away. It's dark lilac and has a joke ghost on the front, basically a white sheet with two eyes. It has a 'Thank you' in white too. Spooky writing. It looks like it was designed on a computer. Inside it says:

THANK YOU SO MUCH FOR TRYING. CHARLIE
IS VERY GRATEFUL. COME BACK TO ST ALBANS
FOR SOME EXTRA HOSPITALITY. I'LL EVEN TAKE
OUT A MORTGAGE AND GET YOU A BOTTLE OF
YOUR FAVOURITE CHAMPAGNE.
NEIL XX

I can't work out what I think about this. In my half-pissed state I'm slightly affronted by the 'funny' ghost, but

I also think the message is really sweet. And from the looks of it, Neil designed the card himself. That's rather cute.

Just as I'm about to move to the living room, Inka darts towards me and curls round my ankles. Then the bulb pops. One minute light, then the next pitch-black, apart from the glow from the lamp-post outside. I heave a sigh and head to the kitchen, then stop in my tracks as a woman in an old nurse's uniform from the calves up walks across from my living-room door towards my bedroom. She's humming to herself – I don't know the tune. Her face is fuzzy, and I can't see details from the side, but she's got a white headdress on and she's wearing one of those longish skirt/white-apron combos. She also has short sleeves with white cuffs at the end and dark tights. I have no idea what shoes she's wearing because the bottom of her legs and her feet don't exist. As I stare in complete incomprehension, her skirt rustles and she disappears through the wall. I don't do anything for about three seconds, then I make a noise in my throat that I've never made in my life: half-scream, half-growl. I look down at Inka, who is standing staring at the exit point of the nurse with her hackles up. I don't even bother saying it in my head, I shout it out loud, 'FUCK-ING HELL, FRANK, WHAT WAS THAT?'

I leg it to the kitchen, switch on the light and, grabbing wine from the fridge, I sink to the floor. My heart is trying to leave my chest by the fastest route.

'FRANK?'

Frank doesn't answer and I remain on the floor, necking wine from the bottle. I'm shaking. Inka, knowing that her mammy isn't happy, snuggles up beside me. This may also be because it's time for her dinner, though at least she's considerate enough not to start nagging me. Not yet.

'Frank, I know you can hear me. And there's a deal – I thought you knew the deal. I don't want to *see* them. I don't mind hearing them or seeing them in my mind's eye, but I am not mentally strong enough to see ghosts walking about my flat, with my own terrified eyes. Or anywhere, to be honest. How am I supposed to sleep tonight? How? You fucker.'

'She wasn't a ghost.'

'So now you pipe up! What the fuck was that, if it wasn't a ghost?'

'The floors have been built higher up since she was alive, hence you couldn't see her feet. She didn't acknowledge or see you, and she was getting on with her life, right? She walked through a wall because there's a new layout to the houses. She used to work at the old infirmary. She was getting on with stuff in her time, not haunting you. She was off on a late shift. She's called an apparition, not a ghost.'

This does mollify me a bit, but I still want answers.

'Why now, though? I've lived here for ages. Why am I seeing her now?'

'Because, scaredy-cat, someone or something has activated you to a much higher level. You're connected to all kinds of spooky shit now. This is going to be fun. So much extra to learn.'

This is not what I want to hear.

'What if I don't want to be connected to extra stuff?'

'You'll be fine – just go with it. Nothing will happen that you can't handle. You've gone up a belt, that's all. Imagine

you're a kung-fu chick who recently graduated to her purple belt.'

This makes me feel rather panicked.

'Maybe I'm still miles back on yellow. Maybe purple's too advanced.'

'Never. Simply breathe through it and look for signs.'

'What do you mean, signs?'

'Byeeee.'

'No-o-o. Are you kidding me?'

Frank's not kidding, he's gone. But knowing that I just saw a film of the past, and that I'm not being targeted by a spectral nurse, does actually help. I'm quite impressed actually. She looked real, if a tiny bit pixellated, and I didn't drop dead from an actual heart attack, so I'm braver than I thought. But still the question remains: why now? I've never seen any rogue nurses wandering around my place before today and I've lived here for ages. I think I need to feed my hungry Inka, then do a meditation to calm down. After that, I'll smudge the place with my trusty sage stick. Maybe the nurse was a sign that I really am 'developing'. Whatever's happening, a quick telephone call to Sheila is in order. She'll put it all into perspective for me, and I need that so I can sleep tonight.

SEX WARS

I've made sure I'm ten minutes early for work this
morning as I don't want any snark from that Maeve.
The Tube wasn't as shit as yesterday, and thankfully
I've had time to buy a gigantic dose of caffeine on the way
in. I did sleep last night, but it was in bursts of twenty minutes with half-hour awake breaks, simply because I'd left
my lamp on and I need proper darkness to sleep. Sheila
tried to put my mind completely at ease before bed, saying
I was obviously 'ready for the next level', but I still didn't
want to see any more spectres wandering around my flat,
so I left the light on. I'm whacked, but I don't think that'll
make any difference. Brett is so self-involved I doubt he
really notices things about other people. My main concern
right now is that my spookiness is through the roof today
and I know, just *know*, that I should be at Cross Bones and
not here, about to suffocate once more under the weight of
two talentless narcissists.

I wave at Tom the super-beard again, who is talking to
the cleaner, a tiny, wide woman with great dimples. Then as

I enter the auditorium, I feel a wave of unspecified hormonal emotion from somewhere. I immediately spot Gerald, who raises an eyebrow as I sit down by him. I look towards the stage and my right eyebrow joins Gerald's in sympathy. Claire, who is playing 'Maeve now' (yeah, right), has shown up in bright-red lipstick, a black shirt, skin-tight jeans and knee-high boots. Not as innocent as I thought then. She's chatting to Brett, who is barely keeping his tongue in his mouth.

Maeve is glowering a few feet away as Peter asks her questions. As soon as she can, she shakes off Peter, turns and says in as measured a voice as possible, 'You look very dressed up for a rehearsal, Claire. Are you off somewhere nice afterwards?'

Claire smiles shyly, an absolute innocent to all the world. Oooh, the cheeky little mare, she knows what she's doing.

'No, Maeve, you said I was playing you, so I thought I'd go for your sexy look and also try to make myself look older. I'm only twenty, so . . .'

Maeve's face flushes puce. Brett, completely oblivious, nods approvingly.

'It works well, Claire – nice one.'

Maeve takes a seat at the front, and Claire and Peter sit in the row just in front of me and Gerald. As they arrange themselves, I pat Claire's shoulder in a friendly way and she turns and smiles. Gerald winks at Peter, who winks back then whispers, 'Do you sense an atmosphere today?'

Gerald nods at him. 'A tad.'

Brett claps. 'Hello, everyone, we'll start with our vocal warm-up like yesterday, then after that I will pass you all a large sheet from a sketchpad and I'd like you to take your primary character. Tanz, in your case that'll be an easy choice, as you only have one. And I want you to draw an animal that represents the essence of that character. Strive deep and think big. Or maybe small, if you decide they're a field mouse, yeah?' He laughs like he just told a fabulous joke.

I hear Gerald sigh and whisper, 'Moron.'

I put out a prayer for escape. 'Frank – someone, anyone – get me out of here.'

Maeve's back is as straight as an ironing board. I can't see her face, but I know she's fuming. This is ridiculous; they're playing out a soap opera in our rehearsal time. I cannot believe the amateurishness of this fucking mess. I wouldn't care, but even though Claire's a sexy girl, we've only been here a couple of days; there's no way she's had anything to do with Brett and his squidgy face in 'that' way. It seems Maeve's losing her nut simply by dint of there being a woman in the room who she feels inferior to, youth- and beauty-wise.

We all stand and form our circle, with Brett joining us when he's pressed the play button. It's pretty similar to yesterday, but with one big exception. Yesterday Claire was in a sweater, joggers and Converse. Today she starts fast-stepping in that shirt – red lips, blonde hair flying and her perfect bazookas bouncing about like they have a life of their own, her shirt open one button too many, like Maeve's was yesterday. (Today Maeve is wearing a bell-sleeved seventies dress with thick tights and brogues; when I glance at her, she's staring straight ahead, stony-faced.)

I can feel the nervous giggles coming on again and I have to suppress them as I watch Brett trying not to look, but very obviously stealing lascivious glances at Claire's boobs. Gerald's shaking his hips again, but wheezing a bit more today. I suspect he's hungover after carrying on at home following our after-work drinks. I'm basically too tired for this shit, but I make the odd gibbon noise and jiggle my shoulders to show willing. Peter's having a whale of a time, fast-stepping and beatboxing. I love him for it.

When the music finishes, Brett lets out one of his triumphant whoops, then gets us all to sit around the table at the back of the stage and, after a ridiculously elongated pep talk, hands us paper and coloured pencils. I tell him I need to nip to the loo, then I run downstairs and make a call outside on the street.

'Bill, this is a disaster. The play is awful, the director is shit and the writer is a fucking twat. The actors are fine, Gerald Birch is a dream, but we can't save this thing.'

'But, Tanz, you signed the contract . . .'

'Bill, he's got us drawing pictures of animals to represent our characters. We're trained fucking actors. The voice warm-up is us bouncing ridiculously around the stage to some cheesy drum and bass. Like kiddy-rave. Another few days of this and Gerald will be in hospital. Can't you do anything to get me out of this?'

Bill sounds immensely displeased with me.

'I'll look into it, but I don't think I can. They could sue you. And it's only two weeks, then a week onstage. It'll put some pennies in the bank.'

'Fucksake, okay. Just don't bring anyone to see it. This

is not going to further my career *at all*. I need to go back up there now and draw a hairless trapped bear.'

Bill laughs. 'That's my girl. Take a deep breath and get on with it.'

I don't want to get on with it, but I slope back up, a bad huff coming on. When I return to the table, Brett is standing behind Claire, admiring her 'drawing'. As I sit, I see her terrible sketch of what looks like a dog with fat legs.

'Nice horse,' says Brett.

'It's actually a rhino,' Claire replies.

Maeve stands up abruptly and walks out. I'm still a bit confused as to whether Claire is doing this on purpose. She must be. I hope she is.

Peter holds up his page. It's a rather cute sketch of a squirrel. I'm not sure what squirrels have to do with his character, but he says, 'I've always liked sketching British mammals.'

I look at Gerald's page. He's drawn the *Titanic*. I kick him and he covers it with another sheet and begins to draw a coiled snake. I quickly sketch a noble-looking cat – it's the best I can think of to calm Maeve down when she comes back in, and the only thing I can really draw quickly. I always doodle cats' faces when I have a pen and paper in front of me. When we've finished our animals, Brett finally registers that Maeve has left the room and not come back, and he leaves us to go and get her. Peter gives a little more shading to the tail of his squirrel, then glances up at us.

'This has nothing to do with my character. But I'm going to get as much fun as I can out of this. Those two are nut-jobs.'

Claire nods and glances at the exit before speaking.

'Maeve pulled me to one side when we finished yesterday and told me I might benefit from some coaching from her to get my acting "on point". She can fuck off. I've been acting since I was five. I just wasn't giving "my all" in the read-through. Everyone knows you don't go for the Oscar in a read-through, the cheeky bitch. She wasn't there when Brett cast me – that's what this is about. She's terrified of other women. She can do one.'

Oh my goodness, these two are about a million times more sussed than I was at their age. This is hilarious!

Gerald claps his hands together and laughs like a walrus.

'Anyway, Maeve seems a bit upset by my outfit today, doesn't she?'

Peter snorts. 'Claire and I have known each other for ages on the circuit. We both went to the British Talent School from age twelve. We didn't think we'd both get this play and, after yesterday, we didn't know if we wanted it any more.'

I'm so impressed. 'You legends! How are you so switched on?'

Claire sniffs. 'My mum was like Maeve, so I left to live at my nan's when I was seventeen. I can smell a jealous lunatic from a mile off. I'm nice to everyone, but that doesn't mean I'm stupid. Plus, I lied about my age. I'm twenty-four, I just look young.'

I can't help it; my admiration is mighty. 'I fucking love you two.'

Gerald clears his throat loudly to indicate that our director has returned. Actually Brett has brought back our writer, who is looking a little less furious, but seems absolutely determined not to look at Claire.

'Okay, folks, take the spirit of your animal and use it today as we begin to stand our masterpiece on its feet. As we're starting right from the beginning, Tanz, and there's that big opening with the God of Judgement, the Paranoia Demon and younger Perdita the Mighty, I don't think you'll be part of rehearsals at all today, though you can definitely stay and watch if you fancy getting some inspiration?'

My heart gives a leap of joy when I realize my prayer has been answered. Gerald looks at me like murder, and I blow him a kiss.

'Thank you, Brett, but it would be nice to go and study my lines elsewhere. Good to be fully prepared, isn't it?'

He nods sagely. 'Of course, so let's say ten a.m. sharp for you tomorrow.'

'And if you have any questions about your character – how to round her out properly, get that extra subtlety – just write them down and, as the writer, I can help you.' Maeve bares her teeth at me. It's supposed to be a smile, but her eyes are hard as a witch's kneecaps.

I smile back at her and nod to Gerald, who's standing behind everyone, miming hanging himself. Claire and Peter both smile at me innocently. The complete tykes.

'Have a ball, my lovely acting *compadres*.'

And with that, I make my escape. In the bar, Tom is sitting at a table, filling in a ledger. He looks up.

'You running off already? Had enough?'

I engage my brain for once before I speak, as he may be friends with those two fuckwits upstairs.

'My character comes in later. It's a lead role, but a bit of a standalone. So, I get today off.'

He glances at the stairs leading to the theatre, then lowers his voice.

'I thought she was going to smack Brett just before – that writer. I couldn't hear what she was saying, but she was very sharp with him. What on earth is going on up there?'

'Sex wars, Tom. That's why I'm single. You start off like two otters holding hands and, before you know it, one of you is an angry wasp with your stinger out.'

He sips at what looks like a pint of orange squash and nods. 'Amen to that.'

CROSS BONES NEEDS YOU

I'm barely out of the door of the pub before I hear a voice in my head. The lass with the soft voice. Fuck, so that wasn't a 'dream' the other night – she's real.

'I think you should go back to Southwark. Cross Bones needs you.'

'Hello, soft-voiced lass. I had a feeling I'd be going there today. Incidentally, who are you?'

'I'm a friend. Frank brought me. And yes, there's something extraordinary going on at the graveyard and you need to get there as soon as possible, as you're involved now.'

'What do you mean, I'm involved?'

'You just are.'

I have no idea why these voices always talk in riddles. Even Frank does it.

'Do I have time to get something to eat? I only had coffee this morning and I'm feeling a bit heady.'

'Of course! You've got to keep your strength up – get those vitamins.'

'Oi, the last thing I need is a bloody fitness guru in my head. I want a big fat pastry with jam. Fuck vitamins!'

I hear a far-off dirty laugh. Soft-voiced lass has a sense of humour. That's good. I call in at a sit-down bakery I know on Chapel Market and get a massive croissant, warmed up, with butter and homemade marmalade. I have it with a chamomile tea, to avoid caffeine overload, and am in absolute heaven. The last thing I'm going to do is look at that bloody play; instead I put on my headphones and listen to some happy music. I also text Neil:

Thank you for the card – even if you are casting nasturtiums on my 'powers' with your cartoon ghost. And not even selling your car would cover the price of my favourite champagne, but thanks for thinking of it :-)

As I dust pastry crumbs off my legs and head back to the Tube, I think of the nurse from last night. It's strange that she would show up now, after my visit to Cross Bones. In fact, since visiting that graveyard only a few days ago, I've started having those weird dreams that aren't dreams – visits or apparitions, or whatever they're called. I looked up the nurse's uniform last night, before I went to my fitful bed, and she was from around 1928, which ties in perfectly with her working at the infirmary that now doesn't exist. I wonder what she was thinking as she walked through my walls? I wonder if she felt something in 'her' house at the same time?

It takes a very short time to get to London Bridge from

Angel Tube. I'm at the graveyard within twenty minutes. Before I've even reached the gates I can feel that something has happened. The air is full of electricity. Always, when there's spiritual energy around, I get a pressure in my chest and at the front of my forehead. This is another level. I can hardly breathe.

Louisa is standing just inside the metal fencing by the gate as I approach, and immediately her worried eyes connect with mine. I go straight in. Heather, the gardening lady, is at the other end again, but this time she's clearing up a walled flowerbed that looks like it's been knocked down. I go over to Louisa, who today is wearing a magenta and gold scarf in her hair and small silver hoops in her ears. The rest of her outfit is very practical; I like her style, keeping up appearances while also staying warm and wearing stout shoes.

'Tanz, someone vandalized our garden. The wall was knocked down, but nobody saw anything. Why would anyone be so mean?'

'Can I have a look?'

'Of course.'

We walk over to Heather, who is shaking her head to herself.

'This makes no sense. I built this wall myself a few years ago. It's like it developed cracks and disintegrated, it's not like it was knocked over at all. That would take quite some work.'

'Hi, Heather, I'm Tanz. I was here the other day; I don't know if you remember?'

She stops what she's doing and smiles at me.

'How could I forget – you and your colourful friend praising our work and meditating on the bench over there. Saying that, when you left, you looked like you'd seen a ghost. I was gagging to ask you what was going on.'

Louisa nods. 'Yes, I sometimes "feel" energies here and I was dying to know what you were doing.'

'You feel them?'

Louisa looks around.

'Yes, I do, and it seems very strange in here at the moment. I can't put my finger on it.'

Soft-voiced lass speaks up at this.

'Tell them. It can't hurt.'

'Ladies, I know I'll sound mad, but the truth is I had seen a ghost the other day. In fact, not one – lots. This place is heaving with them and I don't know why. People don't, as a rule, "haunt" where they were buried. Especially not children and babies. If they remain at all, it's in the places that were most familiar, loved or traumatic to them. Places that made them feel strong emotions. But again today this place is *heaving*. I don't know what's going on, but I'd love to get to the bottom of it.'

Heather scratches her head through her curly grey thatch.

'I don't go in for things that go bump in the night, but I have to say, I thought I heard children laughing next to my ear yesterday. It gave me quite a fright, and Louisa . . .'

'Yes, yes, I saw a man with a shovel. Old, coughing, as I was locking up last week. I stayed and read my book in the little arbour there. It wasn't a cold day and I had my big shawl on, but then I realized I'd stayed too long, and it was getting dark. So, I stood up to leave and I saw him, just over there, half in shadow by the wall. I was about to tell him that he shouldn't be here, and he disappeared. He wasn't looking at me or anything; he was staring at the ground, all forlorn. Then he vanished in front of my eyes. It was rather exciting actually.'

As I'm assimilating this, plus Heather's disapproving glance at Louisa's apparent relish at seeing ghosts, we all hear a scream. We run to the gate and there's a girl in pyjamas and Ugg boots standing outside the large building directly across the road, which I assume contains flats. When she sees us, she flies at us, breathing fast like she's run a marathon. I go out of the gate, and she grabs my arms. She tries to speak, but she's panicking. I disengage my hands and put them on her shoulders.

'It's okay, just breathe, come on, slowly: in for five, that's it, out for five. And again . . .'

She has her hair in a scrunchie and there's a pen shoved behind her ear. She looks like a student to me, with her nose ring and dip-dyed locks, but looks can be deceiving. She's now calmer, and Louisa and Heather have joined us on the path outside. I can feel her shaking.

'Are you okay? What happened?'

She finally composes herself. 'I . . . It's my day off. I was filling out forms for work – I lecture in schools, there's a lot of paperwork . . .'

She looks back towards the building.

'That's my window just there, ground floor, with the plant: look, the aloe vera plant in the red pot.'

Heather nods. 'I love my aloe vera plant. Great for burns.'

The girl attempts a smile, but still looks petrified.

'So, I'm at my table next to the window, filling out forms with my big cup of tea, and I hear a sound and . . . and . . . I look behind me and there's an old woman sitting there in a wooden rocking chair, knitting. An old-fashioned woman, sort of see-through but real, sitting there singing something in *my flat* in a chair that doesn't exist. And I screamed and spilled my tea everywhere and she looked up into the air – not at me, into the air – and said, "Jesus in heaven, what was that?" So I ran out, still screaming. I mean, am I mad? How can that happen? I've lived here three years and I've never ever seen anything like it . . .'

She's starting to panic again. I put my arm around her.

'Come on, I can help you. Let's go and take a look.'

She stands resolutely still, hands still shaking, eyes suspicious.

'What do you mean you can help me?'

'Sorry, I know it sounds weird, but I investigate strange occurrences like this, that's why I'm at Cross Bones. Research. I promise I'm not a robber. We can leave your front door open and everything, so you can shout for one of these ladies if I misbehave.'

She reluctantly turns towards her flat.

'Okay. Just don't make it worse.'

I don't even know what that means, but I take her arm and we cross the road together.

'Promise I won't.'

We're almost at her door when she stops and stares in my face.

'Wait a minute, I recognize you. Are you on telly?'

Fucksake.

OLD KATH

I t's a nice place. Small, but with a lovely big window overlooking the street. There seem to be a lot of *Star Wars* figurines around – she must be a collector. I'm guessing the fireplace doesn't have a working fire as it's got a big half-burned candle standing in it. There are papers on the table covered in tea, the laptop is closed and looks like it missed out on a soaking, thank goodness. The woman is called Fay, it turns out, and she doesn't look that comfortable standing in her own living room right now. I must say, it's teeming with energy. Sheila would love this. I've told Fay I get mixed up with 'that actress' all the time and that I'm called Jen. *It was the first name I could think of, okay?*

'Fay, I'm going to sit on that chair by the window and close my eyes and see if I can pick up on anything. I, erm, work with energies; it's my job.'

'Do you need me?'

'Not really. Why don't you get yourself another cuppa?'

'Okay. Do you want one?'

'Oh, no thanks, I'm fine.'

When she's gone, I do as I said I would and sit on the wooden chair with the black padded seat. There's tea on it, but I wipe it with some tissues from my bag. I face into the room, as Fay did when she 'heard' the woman, and I close my eyes. Immediately I can feel someone else is here and I'm surprised at how well I can 'see' with my mind's eye. There's the woman sitting in a rocking chair, hands knitting away, breasts almost resting on her thighs within a dark, grubby dress. She has a lot of teeth missing, wears a woollen cap on her head, probably one she knitted, and keeps up a barrage of friendly chatter with herself. Even though her words sound slightly distant, they are clear.

'*Course you're hearin' things, Kath, with all them goings-on over there – would disturb any number of the bleedin' departed. Plantin' bones upright, old Jim was saying, plantin' bones in the soil, throwing 'uman skulls at 'em like skittles. 'Nuff to raise an army of the dead. They need t'close it down, we've said 'n' we've said. That miasma's killin' us, an' that devilish reek. They'll have us all in a box at this rate . . . Leavin' God-fearin' folk to rot in the air for all to see . . . no wonder I can hear the screams o' the dead.*'

I open my eyes when there's a noise from the door. No spectre this time; it's Fay, obviously less scared now, making a fearsome racket crinkling a bag of crisps, then opening it and crunching like a gibbon on a fistful of fried potato slices. I grit my teeth. I cannot bear eating noises. I need to get out of here pronto, before I pick up the chair I'm sitting on and lob it at her face.

'So, Fay. You didn't exactly see a "ghost". She's not

haunting you *per se*. She's just sitting there in her living room in her lifetime, doing some knitting and talking to herself. If you see her, you're seeing someone who would be terrified if she saw you.'

'How do you know?'

Fay's speaking with crisps in her mouth. A few crumbs escape. This is pretty much my worst nightmare. Give me ghosts all day, but don't give me someone who eats like a fucking Neanderthal.

'I saw her too. I think, for some reason, the graveyard and its environs have become a bit "active". I'm not sure why, but you can protect yourself: simply imagine a light around you and "ask" whoever "guides" you to close down your perceptiveness so that you can't see anything else that'll scare you.'

I don't even know if this will work, but right now I don't care as I have to get out of here. How can anyone eat like that? Fay puts more crisps in her mouth.

'You are her off the telly, aren't you? You're not called Jen at all.'

I make my excuses and leg it. I hate people.

DEATH-PERVERT

A reply from Neil the police-child arrives as I walk up the road to my flat. I'm listening to loud music, as I am finding it hard to settle my brain. There are ghosts bloody everywhere around Cross Bones. I'm working in a very bad soap-opera situation and very soon I will have to go onstage and pretend I'm not embarrassing myself in public, for a whole week. For good measure, I'm pretty convinced I'm living the 'wrong life', even though I don't know what the 'right life' is supposed to be. Oh, and there's also a spooky nurse wandering around my flat and it seems I'm now a purple belt at 'seeing things that I was promised I'd never have to see'. I want a distraction, but even getting uproariously drunk is off-limits when I have to be at work at 10 a.m. tomorrow. I mean, I saw the state of Gerald today. Hangovers are not a great thing when you have to leap about like a total twit at ten o'clock in the morning.

Neil's text says:

Shame you're not around. For some reason I'm finishing at 4 p.m. today. We could have discussed more ghostly stories over a cheeky pint.

This curveball brings me up short, as I realize I really would rather like the distraction of the company of an attractive man who seems to fancy me. I know how needy that makes me, but hell, I embraced the fact I'm a need-bag a long time ago. Also, I have to let Neil know about the absolute absence of any 'feel' of his friend's sister in the Cross Bones area. It's like there's not even a trace of her energy on the street where her boyfriend lived, which would suggest she isn't dead at all. And Sheila feels the same, so at least it's not only my say-so. This brings me to the conclusion that Charlie looking for his sister has led me to the real mystery – the sudden ghosting of Cross Bones Graveyard.

Is there free parking outside yours? If I can park for free, I can be tempted to partake in two flutes of nectar at whatever ridiculous local hostelry you have.

Neil's sent me his address before I'm even through my front door. *Keen.*

I have time for a shower, a toasted buttered bagel and a cat snuggle before I jump in the car. There's a half-finished cappuccino in my drinks holder that has gone mouldy, so I jump out, throw the minging paper cup in a bin, then jump back in again. A slightly jammed journey up the wet M1 and I'm outside a purpose-built block on a pretty back street in St Albans by 4.20 p.m. I don't always like modern builds, but this one looks okay. Neil emerges from the communal entrance and beckons me.

I'm obviously not the only one who's had a shower and a spruce. His hair's damp – I can see it from here. He's wearing a dark shirt, which is expensive-looking, and he seems very pleased with himself. Probably didn't expect me to jump in the car and drive straight over, on the strength of his message. I had no idea what to wear, so I ended up putting on my jumper dress with the deep V-neck and buttons down the front. It's quite figure-hugging, but not pornographically so.

'Come in a mo, while I fill out your parking permit. You know your registration number off by heart?'

'Cheeky bugger – do you know your own surname?'

I follow him in. It's all new, with gleaming white walls and no dust. You can see how ordered he is by the way his shoes are arranged on the shoe-rack. I follow him into the living room, which is bright with lots of natural light. He has a giant TV, like pretty much every bloke I've ever met, but also has a shelf of books – proper books – which is less like every other man I've met. He has a large, framed *Taxi Driver* poster on the wall above a big maroon sofa, and he actually has a big translucent vase with lilies in it. He bends over a nice pine table with matching chairs against the far wall, obviously his 'dining area', and begins to scratch off the dates on the permit.

'You'd be surprised how many people don't know the reg of their car, Tanz.'

'Well, I'm not one of them, Detective. Nice flat, by the way. Very tidy. You put me to shame.'

He hands me the pen.

'Put your reg on there. I'm very tidy, my mum taught me well. Plus, it's easier to wind down after work in a tidy flat. Now, put that in your car and you'll be safe. Restrictions stop at 7 p.m. anyway.' He pauses for a second, like he doesn't know if he should say the next bit, but then does. 'I've got some really nice red wine in the kitchen if you want to have one here, you know?'

He looks a bit shy. I shrug.

'Okay, nice. Easier than walking to the pub in the drizzle. I'll just pop this on the dash.'

A few minutes later I'm back in his living room with a gorgeous long-stemmed wine glass in my hand, brimming with the darkest of red wine. I'm sure there's more than my permitted driving units in this one glass, but I won't say anything. I'll merely sip and not finish it. We sit at either end of the big, sumptuous sofa.

'Thanks for this, Neil, it's so nice to have an escape.'

'Escape? What are you escaping from?'

'How about my new job is horrendous, but I can't get out of it, I keep seeing ghosts everywhere, and I don't know if I want to be an actress any more. For starters.'

'Bloody hell, that's a lot.'

'Oh, and there's a spooky nurse in my flat.'

'*A what?*'

He looks scared. I don't blame him. I was genuinely scared when I saw her.

'I would really like to think about something else for a

couple of hours. And, well, you're surprisingly funny and actually not a child, like I thought you were.'

'I'm not your kind of bloke, though, am I? I bet you like those edgy lads who love rock music. Saying that, you might be surprised by my music taste. All my tastes actually – I'm not your "typical" copper. And I have to say, you look gorgeous in that dress.'

I bend forward to put my glass on the floor. I sense Neil's eyes shift to the top button of my dress as I move. He darts his eyes to my face again, hoping I didn't notice him eyeing my cleavage. But I did notice, and I don't mind actually, and in a matter of seconds I've crawled to his end of the sofa, taken his face in my hands and am kissing him fiercely. Gratifyingly, he returns my ardour. His kiss is so hot it takes me by surprise, and God, do I need it. Unbuttoning his shirt sends me crazy; this is not the chest of a little boy. Turns out Neil is quite the fully grown man after all. And I seem to be not wearing my dress any more. And boy, oh boy, it only gets better. All I want is to lose myself, and Neil seems very happy to take me away.

We spend two hours like this, mostly on the wonderful giant settee. It rapidly becomes 'The Island of Escape'. By six thirty Neil's in a rather dapper charcoal-grey hooded dressing gown and I'm in his white bathrobe, both still on the sofa, sipping the glasses of wine we abandoned.

'Did you come here to completely destroy my innocence?'

I snort. 'Jesus, there's nothing innocent about anything you just did.'

'Changed your mind about me being a little boy?'

'A bit.'

Truth is, I'm very happy, though I'm not telling Neil that. He didn't get scared and he matched my passion. My head gets so full of stuff sometimes, I really need to decompress from it. Nothing takes me away from life's rubbish more than sex, but I simply don't get enough of it. I'm too picky usually. I bite back a cheeky smile. Have I become a femme fatale?

Neil goes to his ever-so-tidy kitchen and brings the bottle of wine.

'I think you can have a tiny bit more, young lady.'

'I've got to drive home. You're so naughty.'

'Only a drop. It's been a couple of hours now. And I have to tell you, you've completely surprised the Dorian Gray of St Albans. I was going to go to the gym tonight, but I certainly don't need that now.'

'Just so you know, it's not my usual thing to show up at a bloke's house and jump him.'

'Really? You should do it more often.'

He puts a small top-up in my glass, leans forward and kisses me warmly on the lips. Given the chance, I'd go for at least another two hours of naughtiness, but I do have to be up at a reasonable time tomorrow and I'd be knackered.

'Tell me about your scary nurse, please? I'm intrigued.'

I describe the apparition last night, plus the strange stuff that's been going on around the Cross Bones Graveyard since I went looking for Jill, Charlie's sister. I let Neil know that in the absence of any energy at all, I doubt Jill is the real story here, and I believe she'll show up again one day or it'll be found out that she died somewhere else. I then

spout off about the idiocy of my latest job. He pops a spin-
ach and ricotta pizza in the oven as I bore on, and soon it's
eight o'clock and we've eaten pizza and are snuggled into
each other at his end of the sofa.

'Why did you become a policeman?'

'My parents let me watch *Cracker*.'

'But he wasn't a copper. He was a criminal psychologist.'

'Well, thanks for that, because I hadn't realized.' He tuts
and shakes his head. 'I reckoned if I became a murder
detective, then I would suddenly show a spark of genius
when it came to working out who might have done the
deed. Then the top brass would realize they had a natural
profiler on their hands, and I would be like Paul Harrison
and—'

'Paul who?'

'Paul Harrison. He rose through the ranks as a bobby,
and now he's known as the UK's "Mindhunter". Ended up
working with the FBI's pioneering Behavioral Science Unit
for six months. Met a huge number of the world's most
notorious serial killers and is known as an expert in the
field. He writes books about it now.'

'Fuck me, you never told me any of this.'

'Not everyone wants to know about it. Plus, you got
kidnapped by a killer, so you mightn't have wanted to even
think about this stuff. Now that I know you're a death-
pervert, it feels all right to talk about my favourite subject.'

'Oh my *God* – a death-pervert?'

'You know what I mean.'

I don't know if talking about murderers and profiling
should make me feel so much closer to Neil, but it does.

He's certainly not what he looks like. Though right now what he mostly looks like is dessert.

It's ten o'clock before I finally untangle myself. Neil makes me a tiny espresso with his posh machine, to freshen me for the half-hour drive home. I'm showered and in bed by midnight, totally shocked by what happened, and by the fact that I may have felt the tiniest connection with Neil. I'm trying so hard not to care, but he's so much more interesting than I let myself believe. Fighting off darts of warmth for the man I ravished means that I hardly spare a thought for the spooky nurse. I'll bet she didn't have a night back in 1928 as filthy as I just did. I need sleep. The lamp goes off and my eyes wink shut within minutes. Bliss!

VOMIT, SHIT AND REGRET

When I wake up, I'm not in my bedroom. I don't know where I am – it's a dark place, with hay on the floor and people lying everywhere. *Not bliss after all.*

There are groans and sounds of vomiting. I can't hear men, it's only women. I'm lying on my back, and I feel a rush of vomit coming. I 'know' that the rudimentary toilet at the other end of the room is blocked, and I have nothing to be sick into. As I heave, my bowels let go at the same time.

My stomach is cramping, my limbs are aching, I'm desperate for water and I feel like I'm going to die. It's a helpless, hopeless feeling. Everyone around me seems to be in the same state as I am, and my feverish brain keeps seeing rolling countryside. I'm desperate to get back somewhere, but I don't know where that is. The heartache is almost as strong as the physical pain. *What is fair about this, what is fair?* keeps running through my head.

I want this dream to stop now, so I try to make myself

wake up, but the pains keep coming and I begin to cry. Did the poor woman die like this, in a dark room full of vomit and diarrhoea? How could anyone be allowed to suffer like this?

I seem to lie there for hours, trapped in a world of vomit, shit and regret, until finally I make myself wake up. The first thing I do is crank open the window on a damp and chilly morning and suck in the air. That was absolutely horrifying and, considering the fabulous evening I just had, it was a bit of a rude reintroduction to anxiety. My heart is pounding. Soft-voiced lass pipes up in my head. It's weird how she speaks to me more than Frank, and I don't even know her.

'*Sorry about that, but someone really needs to talk to you.*'

'Talk to me? I don't mind being spoken to – you're talking to me now. But throwing me into the bodies of dying people from the past while I'm trying to get some rest is not fucking talking to me; it's harassment, that's what it is. Someone is trying to give me panic attacks while I'm asleep. That's not exactly friendly, is it?'

I hear that dirty laugh again. Soft-voiced lass likes a giggle.

'*It's not all sleep-harassment. The lady in the rocking chair yesterday wasn't scary, was she? She was great.*'

'Yes, she was okay; the fucker with the crisps was the real menace in that flat. But still, there seem to be a lot of funny goings-on right now.'

'*When you get a chance, look up cholera in the work-houses in the nineteenth century. That's what you just saw.*'

'It was hideous. Poor sods. She was in agony. Who was she?'

'It'll become clear. You'll work it out.'

'Me? Mate, I'm currently navigating the job from hell, and my burgeoning alcoholism. I'm not sure how much of a Miss Marple I can do on a bunch of poor people from the nineteenth century. To be honest, I wouldn't even know where to start.'

'I'm not sure you have much choice in this.'

'For Christ's sake. Well, thanks for the heads-up.'

'Frank said you were funny. And grumpy.'

'I'M NOT GRUMPY.'

FULL ENGLISH

The rehearsal room is kicking off when I get in. It's ten to ten and Gerald is giving Brett a loud talking-to, and Maeve has got Claire in the corner and is hissing something in her ear while trying to look like she isn't.

'It should not take a whole day of rehearsal to stand up two pages of text, young man. Especially not those two pages – nothing *happens*. We cannot spend the fourteen days we have for rehearsal discussing every syllable back-wards and forwards to the far end of a *fart*.'

Brett puts out his hands placatingly, like he's Jesus.

'Gerald, man, we've got to bring the chill back to the room. I have my methods; I know what I'm doing . . .'

Gerald notices me.

'Oh, Tarnia, hello. We got two pages done yesterday, in case you were wondering why I look like I already need a drink and it's not even ten a.m.'

Peter looks at me from the stalls, chewing on his middle

knuckle, then casts a meaningful glance towards Claire and Maeve.

I pat Gerald on the back as I move towards the actress and the writer. 'Gerald, you always look like you need a drink.'

Thankfully he laughs at my joke. Brett claps his hands, but I ignore that and reach the girls. Claire is wearing a velvet catsuit in dark navy, with flat little trainers. She looks glorious, with her blonde locks and perfect, dewy skin. Maeve, with her olive complexion, dark hair and cowboy boots, plus a frilly blouse and silver skirt, is also as glam as hell, but overdoing it, and actually it's exhausting looking at the pair of them. I don't have the time or inclination to make myself that perfect each day. Looking naturally flawless takes me hours, as does glam. That's why I go for shabby chic. As I reach them, I catch the end of Maeve's sentence.

'... if you put half the effort into actually being good onstage as you do into trying to make Brett fancy you, we might have got more pages done yesterday.'

Claire glances at me as I reach them, and Maeve stops talking, turns and gives me one of her dead smiles.

'Sorry, Tanz, private work chat going on here.'

'Well, Brett has clapped his hands, so I think we're about to start.' I take Claire by the elbow and lead her away, whispering, 'Fuck, you look amazing. Are you okay?'

She whispers back, 'I fucking hate her. I'm coming in naked tomorrow.'

We sit and wait to hear what joy Brett has in store for us today. I nudge Gerald with my knee and he sighs, shakes his head and mouths, 'He's a cunt.'

Much as I like these actors, this whole thing is stressful. It takes a lot to build up any kind of a positive reputation in the business, and it only takes appearing in one terrible piece to destroy all your hard work. None of us wants to be here. And if only two pages were covered yesterday, then we're not even going to have time to rehearse properly.

Maeve moves to sit down in the front row, throwing a frankly filthy side-eye at Claire as she does so.

'Now, everyone, I know you feel we went over the two pages a lot yesterday, but there's method in my madness. You will know this show inside-out by the time you go onstage – every syllable will be emblazoned on your brain, and you'll be able to fly!'

Gerald laughs. 'Fly with a whole twenty-eight pages out of fifty, because that's as far as we'll have got if you keep working at a snail's pace.'

Brett gives him his best 'stern' look, which isn't very stern. Brett will never be the kind of man who inspires fear in people's hearts. Though he does seem to inspire horrendous jealousy, if Maeve's anything to go by. I don't understand it in the slightest. Showing my age maybe, or possibly just no longer attracted to absolute twats.

'I think you need to respect the process, mate.'

'I have been respecting the process for forty years, "mate", and this isn't going to work unless you step up the pace and stop involving your girlfriend every five minutes.'

Maeve's head snaps round at this.

'What's that supposed to mean?' Her voice is like a car

alarm going off. Her sharpness slices into the middle of my brain.

'Gerald, Maeve is the writer, not my girlfriend. I don't have a girlfriend.' He glances towards Claire. Maeve flushes crimson. 'I'm trying to allow the person who wrote the play to help guide us. They're her words.'

'Young man,' Gerald replies, 'there's a reason why directors often ban the writer from rehearsals. Some keep quiet and observe, then speak to the director privately as and when they need to. They are the *good* writers, and even then, directors don't like their interfering. Others stick their beak in every thirty seconds, because they're unprofessional and need attention and do nothing but disrupt the *process*.'

I'm gobsmacked by Gerald's brutal honesty, but he's not wrong.

Maeve jumps up, grabbing a plastic bottle of Lucozade that she's been drinking from, and lobs it at Gerald. He ducks and it misses. That's when I stand.

'Maeve, what the *fuck* do you think you're doing? This is a rehearsal room, not the school playground.'

'He started it. How dare he speak about me like that? I wrote this, my *dad* has financed this – I have every right to be in the room.'

Brett says nothing, but looks like a landed haddock, opening and closing his mouth. I'm not having this.

'Maeve, I just heard you speaking to Claire like shit. She is trying to do her job, and you are disgustingly jealous because you think she's trying to steal your man. A man who says he's not your man. This is *not* how to rehearse a professional show. How can we work under these conditions? We're the ones who'll look like idiots, once that curtain goes up.'

Both Gerald and Peter shout, 'Hear, hear!'

Maeve turns to Brett. 'Say something! We are a couple. I don't know why he said we're not.'

'Maeve, darling, we've been having a beautiful fling. That's not a relationship.'

'So I'm nothing, and you're already looking to the next one? Is that why your tongue's been hanging out every time Thicko over there shakes her tits around? It can't be her acting you admire – she's *shit*.'

Oh dear. It takes Claire four seconds to spring out of her chair, reach Maeve and swing a punch at her face that Mike Tyson would be proud of. Maeve lets out a scream and crumples to the floor. She isn't knocked out, but I think I see blood.

Claire turns to Brett, lifts her middle finger and calmly enunciates, 'You can keep your shitty play, you absolute knob.'

Peter goes out after her, hand over his mouth, eyes alight with the drama of it all. Gerald is biting his lip, trying not to laugh. Brett gets on his knees next to his furious 'fling', whose nose is as red as a rosehip and bleeding from one nostril. I wish I was back at Cross Bones with my spooks. Far less drama.

I look to Gerald. 'You fancy a full English?'

'Fuck, do I!'

We run out after the kids. Brett mimes calling us as we leave. I'm not sure I'll answer, if that dickhead calls.

DEBRIEF

There's a splendid builder's caff around the corner from the theatre and, having found Claire and Peter lurking outside the Old Red Lion, wondering if they might get sued for walking out, we're round a table, debriefing. I'm having scrambled eggs, mushrooms and beans with brown toast. I'm in absolute heaven. Claire's gone for a huge sausage bap, Peter's having a cheese omelette and Gerald's got the full English with extra bacon. Peter grins.

'Well, that was quite interesting.'

Claire stirs sugar into her tea. Give her ten years and she won't be doing that any more. The young don't know they're born.

'She's lucky I only smacked her once.'

Gerald wipes at his mouth with a paper napkin to remove a glob of sauce. I appreciate his consideration; it would have driven me insane seeing it there.

'I wish I'd had enough of an excuse to smack that idiot

Brett right in the schnoz. That was magnificent, young lady, you'll go far.'

Claire frowns.

'The thing is, she was horrible, but she didn't hit me first. What if she calls the police or takes me to court?'

'I heard what she was saying to you today, Claire, and I'd testify to extreme provocation on your behalf.'

She looks at me gratefully.

'Maeve really hates me, doesn't she? She said I'm a shit actress.'

Gerald tuts.

'Darling, if anyone in this whole universe is qualified to judge if someone else is shit at their job, it's not her. She's an unprofessional little fool and she's wasted our time with her histrionics. Maeve shouldn't be allowed anywhere near a theatre again, ever, so long as she breathes.'

'Listen, everyone, we need to get some stuff straight here . . .' They all look at me as I cut a perfect triangle of toast, dip it in my beans, add some scramble and chew. 'The question is: do we want to do the play?'

There's a short silence. Gerald breaks it.

'Well, the thing is, I really like you lot. Tarnia here is quite the surprise. TV actresses can be shits, but you're a delight, and you two have restored my faith in young people. But the play stinks to high heaven. I thought a good bit of direction might introduce some humour. But no. We're not even going to get a mediocre bit of direction. Brett is an imbecile.'

The laughter around the table is heartening after this morning's drama. Claire puts up her finger.

'I think I'm sacked anyway, so my opinion doesn't count, but Maeve is a lunatic. I can't be in the same room as her. It might result in a worse injury than a red nose next time.'

I look at Claire, such an innocent-seeming blonde beauty. Fuck me, I wouldn't want to get on the wrong side of her, and she could go either way in this business, attitude-wise, but right now she's hilarious and I grin at her.

'Claire, I wish I'd had your balls at your age. Oh, and your face and your figure in that catsuit.'

Claire giggles.

'Peter and I were scared to meet you because we'd seen you in so much telly. You're a legend. I'm so glad you're nice.'

Peter nods in agreement and takes a sip of his tea. I feel my cheeks heat up. I'm still not great with compliments, especially about my career, when it's dive-bombed so badly over the past few years. Peter points at Gerald, who looks up from his breakfast, two slices of bacon poised on his fork.

'And Gerald, you were in *Moondog Squaddies*, my favourite Brit Indie flick ever. I don't want you to tarnish your reputation with this piece of shit.'

Gerald guffaws and shines like a new penny.

'I knew I liked you, Peter, you come across as a young man of impeccable judgement and taste.'

I pat Peter on the hand.

'Peter, you're obviously talented and switched on, so what made you accept this play after you read it?' I ask, genuinely interested.

'Well, money. I know it's not a fortune, but a little bit towards the rent is always good, but also because it was fringe and so awful that I thought we'd get to play around with the themes and lines – make something of it. I never believed we'd seriously have to follow it to the letter. Claire was the same; we thought safety in numbers, didn't we?'

Claire nods.

'How about you: why did you accept, Tanz?'

'My agent made me.'

Everyone laughs.

'No, truly. I couldn't finish the bloody thing, every time I tried to read it I started thinking of loads of other things I could be doing. It was just . . . well, shit. But then I thought there might be some leeway, script-wise, and my agent said it was a great way to show off that I could act onstage. But it's not, is it? I mean, I really like you lot, but I think we'll be humiliated every night if we let that fucking idiot Brett tell us what to do for a fortnight, then go up in front of a paying audience and try to pretend it's not awful. Can you imagine? I'll end up pissed onstage, I know I will; and if *I* end up drunk onstage, think what Gerald's going to be like!'

Everyone titters and, as they do, an idea comes to me.

'Look, you lot, I'm not sure how this is going to play out, but I reckon we need to find a way to persuade Maeve that what she said to Claire, plus throwing Lucozade at Gerald, might be something we have to report to the police and – more frighteningly for her – to her dad. Then maybe, just maybe, I can find a means for us to work together in another way. Let's all swap numbers now.'

We do so, while still eating our breakfasts. And I, for one, am feeling extremely lucky to be out of that rehearsal room. This is much more civilized.

Until Brett bloody calls and ruins it. Of course he does, the knobber.

MEGALADONIS

'Oh my God, she actually lamped her one?'

    I enjoy doing these video calls with Milo. I can see his lovely face, which is a wonderful thing to behold, though I may be slightly biased. What's weird is that while he's doing these rewrites, he's decided not to drink at all. This hasn't happened in all the years I've known him. I mean, don't get me wrong: Milo's said he's giving up drinking many times – we both have. But neither of us has lasted more than three hours. We don't do abstinence. But now here he is doing exactly that, and my heart swells for him. I wish I was that strong, but right now I'm definitely not.

    'Maeve went down like a sack of carrots, Milo. Nosebleed and everything!'

    His big laugh gladdens my living room. Even Inka purrs when she hears Milo laugh.

    'Look I want to ask you something,' I go on.

    'Ohh, what?'

    'I know how busy you are with your rewrites, but . . .'

'But?'

'You know *MegalAdonis*.'

'The best play I never had produced.'

'Yes. Can I have it?'

'What do you mean by "have it"?'

'I've got no money yet, but I might make something from the box office. I mean, this may come to nothing, but I want to direct it at the Old Red Lion if I can.'

'*Oh my God!*' Milo does a shoulder-dance. He's so dance-friendly these days; this telly job must have really done something to him.

'I can't offer you definite wonga, and that makes me feel ashamed, but I'll do my fucking best to reap you any rewards I can.'

'Shut up! That's fantastic. I never thought anyone would ever see it.'

'Thing is, it might need a couple of tweaks to make it fit the cast I have in mind . . .'

'I don't care – I'll do it. I'll tweak whatever you like. I'm already ploughing through my show edits. I enjoy writing for screen, but writing for the theatre is my thing, you know it is. Having a play on, as well as doing my telly job, would be brilliant. I'm getting paid for that, so I'm okay right now, plus I want to see you direct my show. If it's shit, I'll never speak to you again, of course.'

I'm not sure how I'll make this work, but I'll do my damnedest. The thought of directing Milo's work gives me a shot of excitement that I've not felt in ages. Apart from the shot of, erm, energy that I felt last night.

'Milo, I have something to confess.'

Suddenly he's all eyes.

'Have you? What have you been doing?'

'Remember Neil the policeman, who saved me and Sheila from Creepy Dan the Creepy Murderer?'

'Of course. The cute man-baby.'

'He's not as much of a baby as I thought. I shagged his brains out last night and he's all man, baby.'

'Oh my God, I need to pour a drink.'

'*No!* I don't want to ruin your sobriety.'

'Fuck that, this needs a solid Shiraz. Plus you have ghostly goings-on to share.'

He walks to the kitchen and I see his Chinese-lantern fairy lights and his glass cupboard full of cheeky mugs as he moves the phone. He pours a glass, then walks me through to his sofa again.

'So, you fantastic harlot. Every detail. That's an order.'

BUCKET OF DEATH

I'm in another dingy room, this one with what I presume to be an extended family in there. There are a few sticks of furniture, but the little fire will consume what's left of the wood very soon, I'm sure, because something that looks suspiciously like part of a chair leg is glowing in the hearth right now.

The people in here are so emaciated it's frightening. There are two women, who even in this state look alike enough to be sisters. There's a much older-seeming man, who could be their father, and a younger man who is probably husband to the sister he is sitting closest to, as he now puts his hand on her back while he stares into the fire. There are two tiny children curled up on rags, stirring in their sleep. I have never wished harder that I could give people food. Their skin is sallow and their eyes sunken. The thing that really shocks me about this room is the lack of anything of comfort. The walls are bare and peeling, the floor is hard and cold. The furniture is all but gone, so they're sitting on straw and rags, and the fire isn't warming at all. Even by the standards of drawings I've seen of rooms in tenements in the old days, this is joyless and awful.

A boy enters the room, around thirteen years old, but as thin and sunken as the others. He carries a threadbare bag over his shoulder and a bucket in his hand. He puts it down and produces a cup from the bag, plus a loaf, with two apples.

I 'know', as I look at him, that he's stolen these things and I'm glad – glad he's got away with it. Everyone smiles at him, though they all seem too weak to move much. He takes a bite from an apple, then hands it to the husband, who produces a small knife and chops off slices, then pokes at the children, who awaken and suck on a slice each.

The bucket, though. I look at the bucket as he speaks.

'I went to the standpipe.' Again an Irish accent. He dips in the cup.

I know, as I look, that this is not a bucket of water, but a bucket of death. These weak people will be gone soon because of that water. I know they can't see me, but I implore them anyway: 'Please, please don't drink that water. *Please*. Get water from the next pump – this is cursed.'

The sister without a husband stirs. The pain in her face makes me think she has recently suffered hugely. She looks around her and into the air.

'Did you hear that?'

The older man glances her way.

'Hear what?'

'There's someone here with us, Da. In this room. I can feel them. They said something – a woman said something . . .'

'*Now come on, you'll scare the children, Oonah.*'

'*Da, I heard her.*'

'*We're all hearing things these days, my girl. It's the shock of it all. Losing your sister. And the hunger.*'

Oonah doesn't say anything else, but I can see her trying hard to tune in and I'm shocked. She heard me. How? They're in their time and I'm watching from this time.

I try again. 'Get different water, Oonah. And wash your hands after you tend the sick. Do it every time.'

She gasps, then speaks with her mind. '*Who are you?*'

Her reply amazes me so much it wakes me up. She definitely heard me.

SO MUCH GOSSIP

There's a lot to read about the Cross Bones Graveyard and Southwark, if you care to look. I've woken up before 7 a.m. and for more than an hour I pore over documents that I find online – still in bed, coffee on the bedside table. Inka nestles beside me and I'm glad of the comfort as I read about the terrible things that went on in the time leading up to the graveyard finally being closed down. I read that the old lady in the rocking chair was quite right about gravediggers using human bones like skittles. A poor man visited the cemetery and witnessed this happening, then had the horrible shock of recognizing the skull being used as a bowling ball as his father's (he knew the teeth). The man had been dug back up to make way for more burials. This apparently happened a lot.

I read of the 'bone-house' in the cemetery, which had a grille that people could see through and would get so full of as-yet-unburied bodies that you'd be ankle-deep in liquefying flesh if you walked down into it. There are brutal tales of bodies being brought in, and of people in the surrounding houses and in the charity school that overlooked it witnessing bloated corpses and bits and pieces of humans lying hither and thither. Apparently, the smell was a health hazard in itself, something that would definitely finish me off. They called it a 'miasma', and merely the thought of the daily stench of decaying human flesh . . . how did people live round there?

Then, of course, there were the epidemics. Typhoid, typhus and cholera. I'm fairly sure that the 'bucket of death' I saw in that room was actually cholera-infested water from the local standpipe. I didn't even know why I told Oonah what I did, or to wash her hands. But now it turns out that two of the water companies that serviced Southwark in the 1830s and beyond used water from a part of the Thames that was infested with human faeces and industrial chemicals. They hardly filtered it at all. Certain water pumps notoriously infected huge amounts of the population of Southwark, which was rammed with unsanitary and unsafe tenements. Others didn't.

My eye is particularly caught by an article about the Great Famine and how a huge number of Irish immigrants showed up in Southwark to escape starvation. The famine hit in 1845. People fled from Ireland, and not long afterwards one of the most horrendous cholera epidemics occurred in Southwark. The people I 'saw' last night were malnourished. A lot of these immigrants died because they were already weakened. It makes me feel so sad. And then I read that the dead bodies being piled up in the graveyard would rot into the porous soil, and then the rain would wash the disease into local water sources and wells.

I decide I've had enough for today. There's only so much I can read about miasmas and effluvium before I start feeling sick; plus, the thought of what those poor people went through . . . Sometimes I wonder if those who 'run' the world, and always have, are actually human at all. Because they seem to have been happy to let normal folk die horribly and en masse, with very little help or sympathy, since time began.

I check my phone. I have a couple of texts from Neil. I'm trying not to think about him, but it's hard not to. He wants to see me again, but doesn't want to be pushy, and I find that very sweet. Having someone lovely to snuggle into is currently as pleasurable as having nice sex. Usually I would overthink this stuff, but seeing as the rest of my life is a bit full-on and confusing, having someone like me (and me like them back) is quite the bonus. I decide that playing games or trying to play it cool is pointless, so instead I tell Neil the truth. With humour, obviously:

I really enjoyed our pizza night. Should I bring my world-class spicy chilli next time? x

In the time it takes me to have a quick shower, ready to go to work (Jesus, what fresh hell will I walk in on today?), there is a reply:

That sounds good, but bringing your world-class spicy self would be enough. Name your day x

At least this puts a spring in my step for the journey to the Old Red Lion. I literally have no idea what's going to happen. I need to know if this ridiculous show is going ahead now, although I don't know how it can, if Claire and Maeve have had an actual physical altercation. I mean, are they going to try to recast Claire and make us do it anyway? We have so little rehearsal time left.

When I walk into the theatre, there's only Gerald and Brett there. Gerald and I sit together in the second row while Brett stands before us on the stage.

'Well, my dudes, as you know, it got a bit hairy yesterday.'

What fully grown adult says 'my dudes'? Out of the corner of my eye I see Gerald's mouth twitch. I bite down on my bottom lip, as this is not the time for laughter. Brett's weird little face is as serious as I think it's ever been.

'I called you in because I respect you both a lot and wanted to explain.'

'Where are Peter and Claire, young man? Aren't they getting an explanation too? And where's Maeve?'

'Give me a moment of your time, Gerald, and I shall enlighten you.'

Gerald nods grudgingly. 'Carry on.'

'As you know, there was a bit of a disagreement yesterday between Maeve and Claire. Maeve and I met a month ago at an industry do – well, a little party "by movers and shakers, for movers and shakers" – and we felt we had a good work connection. We also got a bit friendlier than that, but I didn't know she was feeling so . . . *attached*.'

'Brett, I think the rest of us could see from a mile off that she was *attached*, so why couldn't you?'

He looks at me slightly guiltily, but not as guiltily as he should.

'I sometimes forget how much I magnetize women.'

Gerald blows his nose. He gets away with it *again*. How does he do it? The snort of laughter sounds like a trumpet in the tissue. But Brett carries on.

'Maeve feels that Claire was flirting with me. Again, this happens a lot, but I was not meaning to hurt anyone, and I didn't mean for this to mess with our process.'

Oh my God, he actually expects us to buy that Claire was doing the flirting, while completely overlooking the fact that his tongue has almost been down to his knees every time he's looked at her since Monday.

'Anyway, Maeve feels that we cannot carry on with this production with Claire involved and also, sadly, now that she knows that she and I aren't meant to be a couple, she has withdrawn her play and I won't be directing it any more. This is a great shame and not the most mature of attitudes, if you ask me. Work should always be held above flings, as the most important thing in our business. I mean, sex is sex, but work is of a higher frequency. I called Claire about this last night and offered to take her for a drink and explain what's happening, but I think she's too upset right now that the job is over, so she said no. She also said it was pointless to all meet up this morning if we weren't rehearsing any more. Peter evidently agreed with her, because he's not here.'

I'm wondering what any of us are doing here. If Brett

115

could call Claire and explain, why couldn't he call us? Of course, I know the answer to that. The dirty dog was in the middle of a self-made crisis last night and still couldn't help taking a punt at his new target, Claire. He's so bloody obvious.

'So, with a heavy heart, I have to announce that we can't go ahead as planned with this play, but I would very much like to work with you in future, Tanz, as I'm a big fan and we could have a great time on something else.'

That means I've been on telly and could put a few bums on seats at some horrible, unprofessional mess of a show of Brett's. As if I'd even consider it. I notice he doesn't mention Gerald in this future world of work. Maybe he couldn't stand Gerald dropping any more truth-bombs?

'I would like to thank you both for the effort you did put in, and I regret the loss of a show that could have been a triumph.'

Oh my goodness, it looks like he's welling up with tears. What an absolute twat. Gerald and I mutter some placatory nonsense, shake his hand, then leave Brett standing in the auditorium, like Norma Desmond when she's shot her lover and realizes that she has nothing left to live for. It's all I can do not to punch the air as we descend the stairs.

'Fucking hell, Tanz. We're free, but did we really have to travel all the way to fucking Angel to hear that speech?'

I spot Tom, standing at the end of the bar, filling in a ledger.

'No, we didn't, but if you want to go ahead and order us our favourite breakfasts at the same place as yesterday, I can catch you up asap.'

Gerald grins.

'Now that's more like it! Scrambled, wasn't it, with mushrooms and beans?'

'Bloody hell, well remembered.'

'I'm not just a pretty face.' As he exits the front door, I head for the end of the bar.

'Tom, could I have a quick word, please?'

'You can have more than a quick word. I want the gossip.'

As I reach him, a text pings in from Claire:

Hope you're okay? That cheeky fucker asked me out last night. He can cock off.

'Oh, Tom, there is *so much* gossip.'

DRINKYPOOS

I've not been in Purple Haze for ages. It's the same as always, cheerful and Mediterranean-looking, with lovely cocktails and good staff. No one's playing any live music on the little stage tonight, there's nothing set up; it's just holiday-evoking Spanish fluff via a CD and hidden speakers. I bagsy the settee where Pat and I sat on our first official date, before he went off travelling the world, and order two Porn Star Martinis. There's absolutely nobody here but me, though that will change, as the bar only opened ten minutes ago.

Sheila arrives as the drinks are being put down on the table. Her lipstick is shocking pink and she's wearing a loose shirt with a big collar and a long skirt, both in dark crimson. I think she always looks knockout, in her own seventies festival-chic kind of way. She's got her Samsara on, which smells great, and it's lovely seeing her look like her old self.

'Ohh, you've got me a glass of rocket fuel, have you?'

She takes a sip and closes her eyes. 'That's so delicious. We've not been out-out for a drink in ages, have we?'

'No, and it's so nice to see you up and about and all dolled up.'

'There's something lovely about being able to put your lipstick on, have a night out and only need to walk five minutes to get home, Tanz. I don't understand people going off into the centre of town, then having to get the Tube late at night with a woozy head.'

I can't disagree there; I've wasted a huge amount of money in my life coming back from town in a taxi. If my mam knew how much money I've spent on cabs since I became an actress, she'd have a blue fit.

'How's the play going?'

'That's one of the things I had to tell you, Sheila – it's gone tits-up. Don't look sorry, though, as I've never been more relieved. The director and writer are both nightmares. Best bit being that because *they* fucked it up, and not the actors, we still get paid. So, the drinks are on me! The writer's dad won't be happy, as he was funding it, but I reckon he'll write it off against tax or something.'

Sheila looks bamboozled.

'Wow, so that's a result, right?'

I nod and take a luxurious slurp of passionfruit-flavoured yum.

'In which case, nice to hear, darlin'. But I have to say, that's not the most important thing in your life right now, is it? I can feel it.'

'Ohh, what you picking up on?'

'Let me turn over a few cards for you, before anyone comes in. Your energy is so interesting.'

Sheila necks the little side order of Prosecco that comes with the martini, takes out her well-worn deck, which is always wrapped in a silk square, and gives the cards a shuffle. She then gets me to pick three cards and she turns them over: Death, Five of Swords, Ace of Swords. Then she turns over another: the High Priestess.

'Well, I'm feeling a great change in you anyway, Tanz. But it seems that life has taken a more serious turn for you. You're not happy with your work at the moment, and a new direction is coming. Also there's going to be conflict in the very near future – as soon as this week, I think – but don't worry, it'll resolve. You're going to learn new and positive things about yourself, though the ride will get a bit bumpy. From what I can see, the spiritual side of you has ramped right up. That's making you feel a bit dizzy and scared, but it's natural because your psychic energy has gone through the roof.'

'Wow, you're so right. I have been feeling dizzy with it all. And as for the spiritual stuff, I'm having dreams all the time, though they're not dreams, they're visions – they feel real. And last night . . .'

'Yes?'

'I was watching a family; I was in the room with them actually, back in the nineteenth century, and I spoke to them and one of them heard me.'

'What? You psychically linked with them in their time?'

'Yes, and it wasn't a dream. I'm sure of it now. Being

next to you heightens my awareness. They were alive and I was the "ghost".'

'That's marvellous – not that I've ever done it. Where were you?'

'A tenement in Southwark. It's always around the area of the graveyard. Something keeps pulling me back. Plus, this voice keeps speaking to me. A soft-sounding woman. She says Frank sent her.'

Sheila holds her cards and closes her eyes for a second.

'She's a friend, not a foe. She's hiding behind a "curtain", but she's helping you as much as she can. Do you have any idea who she is?'

'She knows everything about the nineteenth century in Southwark, so I'm wondering if she's one of them. One with good hindsight. One who didn't die early and fucking horribly.'

'Tanz love, this is so interesting. I'm proud of you, but make sure you're protecting yourself. This is big-league energetically, and it can get really tiring. When are you going back to Cross Bones?'

'Whenever I'm pulled there. It'll be soon, though. I already have this strong feeling that something is occurring again. Especially since that crisp-munching monster got spooked by the old lady in the rocking chair. It's like something, or someone, is igniting all of these spirits, magnifying them so anyone with a trace of "the gift" can sense them and even see them. Oh, and I forgot to tell you. The nurse . . .'

'What nurse?'

'In my flat, a nurse from the calves up, late 1920s uniform, walked straight through my hall and through the wall.'

Sheila begins to laugh, which turns into a cough, but her usual old cough. I look at her with concern, but she stops and stares back.

'Oi, stop looking so worried. *I'm better*. I'm only laughing because I know how scared you are of seeing ghosts. Were you okay?'

'Of course I wasn't. I thought I was going to have a fucking nervous breakdown. But then I sat on the kitchen floor and had some wine and Frank calmed me down. She wasn't haunting me, she was simply going about her business.'

'Well, it's certainly all kicking off for you, isn't it?' Sheila looks at her now-empty glass.

'Should we get the same again?'

'Why not?'

She raises her glass to the bar lady, holds up two fingers and smiles. The lady smiles back. People like Sheila – she never comes across as pushy or aggressive, just real.

'So, Tanz, now that you've properly seen an "imprint", how do you feel about seeing more? Or do you prefer seeing them in your mind's eye?'

'Oh God, I much prefer hearing them and visualizing them in my head to actually seeing them with my own terrified eyes. But at least now I know I won't die of fright on the spot, if it happens again. Not that I want it ever to happen again.'

'I'm proud of you. You're going through such a rapid change.'

'I don't want this kind of rapid fucking change. I want it so gradual that I hardly even notice it. And what about the voice I keep hearing? She turns up and tells me what's what, when I'm having one of my "visions" about Southwark. You say she's hidden and all that, but why would Frank bring her to me now?'

I lean forward, the drink bolstering the truth that I've been dodging.

'I tell you what I think . . . something's going on. Something is hurtling towards me and it's dark, Sheils, it's pitch-black. There's a jigsaw puzzle assembling in front of my bloody face, but some of the pieces are missing. They've been purposely obscured, I'm sure of it. And I'm not enjoying feeling other people's pain and death in my sleep. That shit is not for lightweights. It messes with me for days afterwards. It's scary. After nearly being killed by that fucker Dan, I can do without feeling so helpless again.'

Sheila looks surprised. Almost as surprised as I am by what just came out of my mouth. She puts her hands on top of mine and closes her eyes. After a while she opens them again and shrugs.

'I can't tell you what's happening, love – it's still in shadow. But I know you're protected. And all I can feel about the soft-voiced lady is that she's a force for good, and there's a great sadness she carried in life. Plus, she likes you. That's it.'

'Well, that's something, I suppose. As for the people I saw last night, they'd run away from the horrible famine in

Ireland. They were so thin. I wanted to hug them all. It was so sad.' I well up as I think of them.

'Oh, sweetheart, they died so long ago. All you can do is channel love towards them. That's it.'

Our new drinks arrive. I love having nights out with Sheila. Two couples come through the door, young and arty-looking, and Sheila stashes her cards before they can see. People have a habit of asking for a reading if they even sniff that you do the tarot.

'By the way, what do you think that conflict is, in the cards?'

'I have no idea, but I'll tell you this – something just hit me. You had a naughty night recently, and it put lead back in your pencil! Oh, you cheeky so-and-so. Why didn't you tell me? Wow, no wonder so much is happening, with all the electricity running through your veins right now. You're a hotbed of trouble.'

'How did you know that?'

Sheila taps the side of her nose, then takes a long draw on her new cocktail.

'Never try to hide things from me. I know everything.' She wiggles her eyebrows at me and we both laugh. 'Now tell me what's going on, you secretive little northerner.'

Having witchy mates is the best.

NORA

I feel like my life has been chopped in half. Cleft in twain. I have my waking world, then I have this other world where I'm supposedly asleep, but I end up visiting different times, places, people and sometimes even different planes of existence – like when I met Mona as an angel, or when I meet up with Frank in the Saltwell Park of my childhood or in deckchairs abroad. That's not really where I am; I'm in some kind of 'netherworld'. I don't pretend to understand any of it, but I do accept it, mostly.

What I don't fucking accept is waking up in my own bedroom, not in a dream, and seeing the nurse again, folding up her clothes in the nineteen-bloody-twenties. Or that's what I think she's doing. She's singing away to herself – I can hear it in a slightly far-off way, which makes it spookier, like I'm in a psychedelic horror movie, and she doesn't disappear after a couple of seconds, like I'd expect. I close my eyes, open them, close them again, open them. She just won't fuck off. Inka is next to me, hackles up to the ceiling, transfixed by this lady as she puts items in drawers and hangs them up. I can't see ghost furniture, only the woman; and this time, maybe because of the gloom, she is not pixellated or faint. She looks solid and even though this is fascinating, it's also really bloody weird. I keep blinking, thinking she'll 'go', but every time I open my eyes she's still there. She has dark hair swept off her forehead and short at the back. She's not wearing her nurse's hat, and she's got those little old-fashioned round glasses on.

I shout for Frank in my head, as I don't know what to do: 'For fuck's sake, Frank. Can a woman not have privacy in her OWN HOME?'

'*She's called Nora.*' Frank sounds amused, the shit.

The nurse turns towards me and looks like she's going to walk straight through my bed, and maybe even through me.

Terrified I yell out, 'Nora, GO AWAY. GET OUT!'

Nora's face drops and her hands fly to her cheeks. I whip the blind open as I see and hear her terrified scream. This is not the reaction I expect from a spectre: she looks scared shitless. Then, as light fills the room, she's gone.

My heart's smacking like a jackhammer. I sit on the edge of my bed.

'Frank, don't you dare bugger off. What's going on?'

'*You're getting good at this stuff.*'

'If this is getting good, then I don't want it. I didn't sign up for *Help! My House is Haunted.*'

'*Poor old Nora was just putting her stuff away. You've traumatized her.*'

'How did she even hear me, if she's an imprint? Her poor face – she was absolutely horror-struck.'

'Oh, she'll get over it. And you weren't an imprint from her end. You were as real as anything. Your energy is sucking towards them, not the other way round, and you scared the living daylights out of her.'

'But why is that happening?'

'You've been activated.'

'Oh, come on, what's that?'

'I can't even explain it properly myself. I'm not as all-knowing as I claimed. Still got more knowledge than you, though.'

'Yes, well, you're privy to more cool stuff than I am. Plus, you're not lugging a meat sack around on this planet. You're flying here and there like a shiny little fairy.'

'I'll fairy you in a minute.'

'Ha, my mam would say that.'

'It'll all become clear.'

'Oh Christ, you're not going all guru-tastic again, are you? I just want to know how much longer I have to put up with Nora scaring the crap out of me?'

'I think you'll find you scared the crap out of Nora. She's out of here very soon – she moves back to her mum's in the next twenty-four hours, as her place is haunted.'

Okay, this does make me laugh a bit. How did I end up being a Geordie ghost? I stroke Inka's back as she climbs on my lap. She was as discombobulated by Nora as I was. It's all very well having a new 'skill', but I don't like the hair on the back of my neck standing up on end while I try to work out whether someone in the flat is a ghost or a burglar. How can I ever get used to this? I can't keep waking up and finding people in my bedroom.

'Frank, I'm not sure I'm good at this bit.'

'You're good at all the bits. Relax. Love you!'

And, of course, he's off. But at least I got a 'love you' out of him.

CROSS BONES JIGSAW

I know before I'm dressed that I'm going to pop to Cross Bones Graveyard again today. I'm still in my favourite silky lounging trousers and big off-the-shoulder jumper, and today's *Homes Under the Hammer* was deeply unsatisfying as one of the lots was a piece of overgrown land that they didn't manage to get planning permission for, so it was still vacant by the end of the show. On top of that, one featured property was bought by an extremely tight buy-to-let landlord, who got the flat as a mess, painted the woodchip wallpaper marigold, cleaned the manky sink and put some rugs down, then rented it out again as a mess. The pure greedy laziness got my back up.

Now I'm getting this gut feeling that something's going on and I need to head off to London Bridge asap. It's backed up by suddenly hearing the soft-voiced lass in my head.

'Chop chop, time to go!'

I'm so used to the idea that something spooky needs resolving in Southwark that I've already selected a book from my 'should have read by now' pile and put it in my bag. Something I can work my way through on my Tube journeys, until I finally figure out what the hell is going on down there.

I put on some sensible walking trainers (sparkly ones – I'm not completely lost to the 'ordinary' side), with my black jeans and a stripy jumper. I put my hair up with a clip and make a flask of coffee from the cafetière. Milo sent me the funkiest little shocking-pink flask yesterday with a flip-top that you can drink straight out of. I'd been moaning at him about the price of takeaway coffees and this was his reaction, the little diamond. I love it. I'm checking my bag to make sure I have everything when the phone rings.

My agent. Oops! I forgot to tell him.

'Hello?'

'Tanz!' Bill's voice is a friendly Scottish boom, so I'm not in trouble. I hear Joe, my other agent and Bill's partner, shouting 'Hiii!' in the background.

'I'm so sorry Bill, I forgot to tell you yesterday about the play.'

'You seem to have got your wish, on full pay. How did you manage that?'

'The writer turned out to be mentally unstable and the director is an absolute melt. The writer pulled out, so it's on her to pay the fees. Please don't ever put me up for anything else with his name attached, or hers.'

'Ohh, you've piqued my interest now.'

'Let's just say there was a huge pile of jealousy going on there, before a single line was read out loud. And two days ago the writer got a smack in the face from an actress. Not me. A young blonde who'd already had enough.'

'Jesus, the drama! Well, at least it's folded. Onwards and upwards. I'll put you up for something much better.'

'Okay . . . erm, Bill?'

'Yes?'

'Oh, it doesn't matter. It's only a thought I had. I'll let you know if it comes to anything.'

'All right. Well, enjoy your day. And speak soon.'

'Thank you, and love to Joe.'

I don't know how to articulate what I'm feeling. Plus, I don't have anything concrete to say about the Old Red Lion, but after a short chat with Tom yesterday, I'm meeting him for a coffee next week and there might be an exciting plan brewing. Meanwhile I have to go, right this second. The Cross Bones jigsaw is revealing more pieces – I can feel it like a battering ram to the gut and the sooner I get there, the better.

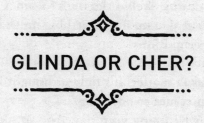

GLINDA OR CHER?

Walking out of the Tube station onto Borough High Street has quite an effect on the front of my forehead. My third eye falls open like a broken fridge door. People are milling about as usual, the sky is pretty clear and, despite a bracing nip in the air and a breeze, everything seems normal, and folk are going about their business. In fact a couple of people are smiling, which is quite a sight in London.

They're not me, though – lucky them – so they don't suddenly feel like they've been caught up in an energetic tornado, akin to the whopper at the start of *The Wizard of Oz*. Speaking of which, in modern terms would I be Glinda or the wicked one? Anyway, as I set off down the road towards Union Street, I notice blanket-man has covered himself completely with his blanket in an unsuccessful attempt to hide himself guzzling from a two-litre bottle of cider. Looking at him all covered up, I get the sense of the 'messages' that I'm meant to be receiving also being covered up. Nothing makes any linear sense in the slightest. I'm so awash with death and sadness from people who left the planet such a long time ago, but I still have no idea why I'm being shown the things I am. I get an overwhelming sense of a second layer of existence going on as I walk past blanket-man, my mind wondering if in his world of drink and basic survival he senses any of this at all, and it makes me feel all floaty. There's a hum in my belly and a pressure in my chest as I turn down Union Street towards Redcross Way.

Soft-voiced lass pipes up. *'Strictly speaking, Glinda wouldn't shag the brains out of a policeman on his sofa – too busy being sparkly and good – but you're not horrible to anyone who doesn't deserve it, so you're not the wicked one, either. I'd say you're more* Witches of Eastwick *than those two. Probably a mix of Susan Sarandon and Cher.'*

'You know *The Witches of Eastwick*?'

'Why wouldn't I know The Witches of Eastwick?'

'I thought you might be a ghost from the 1800s or something. You're so clued up about the times then.'

'Cheeky! How many hundreds of years old do you think I am? Maybe I just studied history, like you do when you look on Google?'

'Oh.'

I stop in my tracks. There's a small crowd outside the graveyard. A man in a beanie hat is shouting and pointing. He's with a couple of friends who are trying to calm him down. Louisa and Heather are there, plus a skinny man with a straggly goatee, also in gardener's greens. I rush over. Louisa and Heather look very glad to see me. Louisa waves and points at beanie-hat lad.

'Ah, Tanz. Can you have a word with this young man? He's very, very upset. His name is Tyler.'

Tyler and his friends look like an extremely well-dressed Grime outfit, immaculate in branded clothes and with perfectly coiffed close-cropped Afro hair. I'd expect to see them on some music channel, not standing on a street in Southwark, shouting into a cemetery.

'I swear down, man. I saw it, right there. I smelled it! I heard it! I shouted for you to come see, turned around and it weren't there no more. This makes *no sense*.'

'Tyler, there ain't nothing there, bruh. Can we go now? This isn't cool.'

The other friend isn't saying anything; he looks scared. I turn to Tyler, pat his arm.

'Are you okay?'

'Yes, I'm okay, but I know what I saw over there, it was . . . there weren't no concrete, it was earth. And mud. I swear down . . .'

'Look, this sounds mad, but I know a bit about the graveyard and things that have been going on. If you don't mind, I'm going to close my eyes for a minute and then I'll tell you what I think you saw. Is that okay?'

Tyler nods, looking relieved that someone believes him.

I look round. 'Everyone, just be quiet for a minute please.'

I close my eyes, facing into the graveyard. I ask the soft-voiced girl what Tyler saw. For a second it comes to me, along with the smell . . . I open my eyes again and everyone is watching me. I look up at Tyler, who must be at least six foot four.

'There was a corpse, over there by the bed with the red

flowers. Only when I looked, I saw overturned earth there and a body, not a flowerbed. It was an older child, and mostly rotted. The head was nearby and there was a woman standing next to it, crying hysterically. I could see her from behind. Horrible and sad. No wonder it freaked you out.'

There's a collective gasp. Tyler does that hand-flick thing that would break my wrist if I tried it.

'See! I told you. She could see it as well. The stink of it . . . How? How did I see it? How do you *know*?'

I smile at him.

'I'm a spooky Geordie witch. My family has a history of knowing things they shouldn't, so I'm stuck with it I'm afraid.'

Surprisingly, Tyler nods like he gets it. 'My grandma was like that. Used to scare my mum.'

'Tyler, that's it!'

'What's it?'

'You've got a bit of what your grandma had. This place is *so* haunted at the minute – you tuned in.'

'Ah fuck, man, am I going to start seeing dead people?'

The frightened-looking mate appears even more frightened and puts his hands on the top of his head.

'Nah man, my dad says his grandma was like that too. Am I gonna see corpses and shit?'

'Well . . . Sorry, I'm Tanz, what's your name?'

'I'm Wayne.'

'Wayne, if you didn't see anything today when this place is teeming, you're probably okay. I don't think everyone inherits the gift.'

'Thank fuck. Oh sorry, sorry, f-word and shit.'

I laugh and shake my head.

'Nobody has to apologize to me for swearing. I've got a mouth like a sailor. Are you okay now, Tyler?'

Tyler is breathing shakily, looking into the graveyard and all around the street. 'I'm better now, thanks, but . . . there's this feeling. I think I need to get away from here.'

'You're picking up on all kinds of stuff, so probably best. If you feel anything like this again and you don't want to "see", take a breath into your stomach and ask in your head for protection. I know it sounds weird, but it should help. Ask your mum about your gran, too. She sounds interesting.'

'I will, Tanz. Thank you . . . thanks.' They're already walking off, quickly.

The one whose name I didn't get looks back at me as they leave.

'You know you look like that woman off TV, right?'

I shrug. 'I wish I had her money.'

He laughs and soon they've turned back towards the high street.

Louisa begins to laugh. Heather joins in, and the lad with the little goatee just looks stunned.

'Okay girls, and boy – sorry, we haven't met,' I say.

'I'm Chris.'

'Well, Chris, this place seems to be a hive of activity at the minute. What have I missed?'

Heather and Louisa look at each other, then at me. Louisa links her arm in mine.

'I think we all need to go for a coffee. Let's lock up for half an hour.'

SOMETHING UNEARTHLY

Chris isn't happy talking about ghosts and ghoulies and says he'll go back to the office and do some admin, while the rest of us visit a coffee shop. I find it very telling that he doesn't stay at the graveyard on his own and carry on with his gardening duties. Just shows how spooked people get.

The others take me to a pretty little Italian place a hundred yards away, where the proprietor obviously knows Louisa. They have a lively chat in Italian while I peruse the menu and decide I want a pistachio cannoli with my cappuccino. I've realized recently that if I fancy eating something, I simply do it, and this is not the proper attitude of an actress – not one of my age. I've also taken to having oat milk in my coffee and I wonder if they're going to think I'm a dick if I ask for it. Turns out they have about a thousand different kinds of milk behind that counter, and Gino (for that is his name) doesn't blink when I request oat.

Heather is a bit discombobulated, and her foot keeps tapping on the tiled floor as she waits for her cup of tea.

Louisa smiles at me as she arranges her coat on the seat behind her.

'Well, Tanz, I think it's lucky we met you when we did. Our little haven has become a hotbed of paranormal activity, hasn't it, Heather?'

Heather pushes a curly grey strand behind her ear and nods to me.

'There's definitely something unearthly going on. I'm not scared exactly, but I'm concerned. When I come in first thing, there's such a feeling of pressure in there. I'm hearing all sorts now, and another of the flowerbed walls has a crack in it. I don't think anyone's breaking in and causing damage, though, not any more. It feels like some kind of *force* is building and it's actually making the ground shift. I mean, I can't explain that to anyone official, any more than I can explain the sound of a woman weeping and screaming the other day. I thought maybe that woman who ran out of her flat when you came last time had come out again and was screaming in the graveyard. But no. There was only me, and it was really quite alarming.'

'What about you, Louisa, have you experienced anything else?'

Louisa leans in closer, once our order has arrived.

'Where the bone-house used to be. I heard a bunch of people, weeping and keening. I looked it up online and instead of having open caskets in their tiny houses, which would stink and cause disease, they would have the coffin open in the bone-house and people would visit. They would cry for their dead there.'

'Bloody hell, and you heard them?'

138

'I've heard them a few times now. And I read that the Irish who came over here to escape the famine all used to want open-casket funerals. Where they lived was really cramped and they had to have a tap on the coffin, to let out all the juices leaking from the corpse, because of how long they would keep the body.'

'I'm eating!'

Heather has an egg sandwich poised an inch away from her lips and has gone a bit green. Personally, I could listen to stuff like this all day, but I know it's distressing for others.

'Sorry Heather. I just thought it would provide some background.'

I take a bite of my cannoli, which is magnificent, and make sure I've swallowed most of it before I speak.

'I've been looking at the history too, since I first came to the graveyard, and I've been wondering: if all these occurrences are happening now, is it an anniversary of some sort? The milestone of a mass death, or maybe the birthday of someone who died tragically? I've read a lot and the history is fascinating, but I cannot think what it could be. The other possibility is that someone's grave was disturbed recently. Has anyone been dug up?'

Both ladies shake their heads. Louisa begins to list what she can think of.

'In 1853 the graveyard was closed for good. There were three cholera epidemics in the nineteenth century up until then, plus a few runs of typhoid and typhus. The Thames Water Company didn't change its practices when asked to, so that killed additional people with contaminated water. But no specific date. The workhouses in the area had some terrible mass deaths, because the people were all crushed in together to work and sleep, but again no specific time – it was something that happened a lot. And I do remember reading that there were times when workhouse folk in the area survived when many people in the surrounding tenements died, because the workhouses had their own water source. Most people had no idea that washing their hands after being near the "emissions" from people with cholera and typhoid could save them. Or even that using a different pump instead of the one nearest their home could save their lives. Because different water companies supplied different pumps.'

I'm still amazed that I told Oonah these things before I'd researched them properly myself. The guidance to help her certainly hadn't come from me, but *through* me.

'Wow, Louisa, I need to go home and read more. I could listen to this all day.'

Heather is still looking a bit sickly as she munches her sandwich, and I suspect she could easily do with hearing less of this. It's all so sad and fascinating, but it doesn't explain why I'm being haunted in my dreams, and why people in the area are suddenly seeing visions.

'How new is this, by the way? You two seeing and hearing things?'

'I first heard the laughing in my ear about a week before you showed up,' Heather tells me. 'Louisa and I have talked about it and even though I wouldn't say these things in public, or even in front of my husband, I think you've been drawn here for a reason. We just can't work out why, can we?'

Louisa shakes her head.

'No. I've racked my brains asking: why now? When the Jubilee Line workers dug up some skeletons in the nineties, surely you'd think that's when people would start getting haunted? But there were no reports of anything. And now ghostly gravediggers and spooky children, and women in rocking chairs across the road, and complete strangers seeing ghostly corpses . . .' She grins at me. 'I love it, Tanz. Isn't it delicious?'

Heather slaps her arm.

'Hey! I don't think it's delicious, and neither do the other volunteers. We can do without the foundations wobbling as well. We can't afford building work, and our walls are falling down!'

'Girls, I know you've only known me a very short while, but I think you're right: I've been sent to help. And I think the next move is to go into the graveyard at night. To see if we pick up anything extra then.'

Louisa rubs her hands together. 'I'm definitely in!'

Heather shakes her head. 'Much as it interests me, that's a step too far.'

'You don't have to come. And as long as we have torches and lock the gate behind us, so that no one else can follow us in, I think we'll be safe. Louisa, would you be happy if I brought Sheila along? She magnifies what I can do and she's a really talented "seer".'

'The more the merrier! I love this.'

'Don't worry, Heather. We'll fill you in on everything that happens. Or Louisa will anyway.'

'Please be careful. A haunted graveyard is one thing, and could even be a tourist attraction, but crumbling foundations aren't small fry. Something big is going on and it seems to be spreading. I would come, but my husband and kids would ask questions – not ones I really want to answer.'

I remember Mona's dead body in the woods, and the knife at Sheila's throat all those months ago. Compared to that, this is a picnic.

'Don't worry, I've been in much hairier situations than this. So has Sheila. Plus, if no one helps, you're going to be swamped with spooks wandering around the place and scaring the staff. I'm happy to help.'

Truth is, I live for this stuff.

LITTLE MAM

My little mam's calling and I'm scared to pick up. She always knows when I'm up to my eyes in ghostly shenanigans and I don't much fancy a telling-off. I'll try to divert her by talking about the play that fell apart – that might stop her in her tracks.

'Hi, Mam.'

'Hello, Tanz. Care to tell me why I'm seeing people in old-fashioned clothes crying in a cemetery?'

Ah. 'What's that, Mam?'

'You know, before you started clarting around with the afterlife, I was quite good at not seeing things in my dreams. I mean, it still happened, but not as much as this . . . I could close it off a bit. Now going to sleep's like a bloody magical mystery tour with dead people.'

'Well, before you start having a go, this is a very interesting haunting. There's no murder that I know of, and it came out of the blue for me as well. I didn't get involved on purpose.'

'So come on, what's it about? They were Irish. A lot of Irish near us when I was growing up. Tinkers—'

She's about to say more, but I stop her:

'If you're about to say something racist, *do not.*'

She sniffs and sounds offended. 'As if I would. Good-looking men as well. Nice eyes. But this lot were thin as rails, scruffy and crying around a coffin. There were bones and blood and all sorts around them. I needed a cup of tea to settle me nerves this morning.'

My mam always has two mugs of tea after she gets up – nerves or not – the fibber.

'It's this cemetery near London Bridge called the Cross Bones Graveyard. I accidentally saw things when I visited. It's been around for hundreds of years. The priests used to bury these prostitutes there, called the Winchester Geese. They'd pimp them out, then bury them in unconsecrated ground afterwards.'

'Of course they would – shitty priests. Them and nuns, I'd shoot the lot of them.'

'*Mam!* Anyway, later it became a general paupers' grave-yard and as it was really poor around there and rammed with people dying of cholera and all sorts, they got buried in this tiny graveyard. They'd dig bodies up to bury new ones, because it brought in revenue for the parish. There were apparently bones and flesh and all sorts around the place. And a lot of Irish showed up in the area after 1845, because of the Great Famine.'

'Well, I tell you what, our Tanz, if you ever get sick of acting, you should be a history teacher. You certainly know your facts.'

My mam doesn't 'do' computers, which is a shame because I think she'd like reading about this stuff.

'Get Dad to do a printout for you later – "Cross Bones Graveyard". It's so interesting.'

'Well, it sounds it, but what's it got to do with you?'

'I'm not sure. I only went for the first time less than a fortnight ago, looking for a lass who had disappeared. And it's gone from me feeling something weird, to going with Sheila and seeing all kinds of stuff, to my dreams filling with people from the old times in Southwark, to people in the flats around the graveyard – plus staff and people walking past it – seeing ghosts and apparitions and all sorts. I think there's something that I'm meant to solve or put right, but I don't know what.'

'Will you be careful, please?'

'Of course, but to be fair, I'm not sure there's anything dangerous. How about instead of freaking out about it, you keep me posted if you get any feelings or dreams that could offer me an insight? You can be my spook insider? My ghost spy?'

Mam laughs. 'As long as it's not horrible, like that black angel hanging over you. I didn't like seeing that. Nearly got you killed, that little adventure.'

'But it didn't, and I'm much more careful now.'

'Hey, wait a minute, when does that play start that you're doing? Aren't you meant to be at work?'

'Well, before you panic, I'm getting full pay, but no, it went wrong and I'm glad, because it was rubbish.'

'You're getting paid anyway?'

'Yup.'

'What a funny world you live in.'

'Don't I just?'

'Your nanna's been asking after you, by the way. She's got a bad knee again right now, and her eye's gone all misty. I haven't had your dad back in time for tea for three nights running, with him traipsing back and forth for prescriptions, and fixing cupboards and taking her fruitcake because she doesn't like the Madeira cake I got her. I tell you; my nerves can only take so much of this . . .'

Oh Christ, she's got onto the subject of Nanna, and if I don't get her off that track pronto, this monologue will be longer than that awful play I've escaped.

'Mam, you know what she's like: she's old and she's fishing for company. I mean if you want Dad home, maybe you should pop along one day instead?'

'*Me*? Do you know how busy I am? I have a routine. If I mess with that, everything goes to pot. Anyway she's not my mother, and she lets me bloody know it as well. I see her on Saturdays at three o'clock with your dad – that's enough.'

'Well, there you go then. Dad going round there this week is saving you the hassle. How about you cook tea half an hour later than usual, and then Dad won't be late when he gets back; he'll be early?'

My mam makes a strangled noise. I only asked her to mess with the time she makes their food. It's been five o'clock since 1976 and I've overstepped the mark . . .

'Sorry Mam, it was just a thought.'

'I'd be starving by half past five, and I'm not changing anything for her.'

'Of course. Well, listen, Mam, I've got some stuff to do, so I'll have to run. Tell Nanna I'll see her as soon as I can, and give my love to Dad.'

'I will. And you be careful. Not all the stuff you're doing at the minute is about ghosts. There's a reckoning coming for someone who's still alive. They're carrying a secret, but it's going to come out. That's all I can tell you.'

'It's not a woman with red hair, is it?'

'No. I don't think it is.'

'Bloody hell, and you say *I'm* spooky?'

'Difference is: I don't *like* it, pet.'

EXTREMELY LONELY

I decide to walk up the steep road to Muswell Hill, get my glutes engaged, plus buy some bits and pieces of shopping at Sainsbury's via a cafe up there that does great croissants. It's not a cold day and, as I walk, I enjoy the warmish air and the sound of crows cawing as I veer off the main road and wander through the Collins houses of the Rookfield estate. I love that the roads are privately maintained here and, as there isn't direct access to anywhere, the traffic is minimal compared to much of the rest of London. Also, the houses are cute and all different from one another.

It takes me a minute to realize as I walk that there are tears running down my cheeks. In fact I'm sobbing. *Shit!* I cross the road to avoid a dog-walker and sit on a low wall in front of a lovely little house with green window frames. I put on my sunglasses to look less conspicuous as tears flood my cheeks. The feelings are so overwhelming – loss, sadness, love, yearning – and I know this could be hormones, but I'm pretty sure I'm feeling someone else's emotions. I wonder who it could be, but thinking of the sad things I've been linking into recently, it could be any of those poor sods who lost their lives all those years ago.

I close my eyes behind my sunnies and ask to see who I'm tuning in with. Instead of seeing a person, I'm suddenly looking at a view over buildings. I'm high up and a bit dizzy, and it all looks unreal. I sit back heavily on a thread-bare sofa and feel the breeze catch my hair. *Why is this sofa outside?* I suddenly know, with certainty, that this is the end and I'm going to die. Out of the blue, I want to live. I've not felt properly connected to my life for a long time . . . Now I'm ready to stay. But it's all going black and, despite finding some fight in me, it's not enough; I realize it's too late and this is where it stops. The end . . .

I wish I'd known how precious it all was. I wish I'd enjoyed living.

The vision disappears.

I open my eyes and I'm crying, and an old man has stopped next to me. He's wearing a trilby and a brown mackintosh. He looks awesome.

'Are you all right?'

I take off the glasses and wipe away big tears on my sleeve.

'I'm so sorry – I'm fine. Sometimes it just gets a bit much, doesn't it?'

He smiles kindly. 'Oh yes, it certainly does.'

I smile back. 'Thank you for caring.'

I have no idea who I was channelling then; the voice was hard to catch and indistinct, but the passion was real. Such a mix-up of confusion and despondency with a sudden will to live. Perturbed, I walk up to my favourite cafe as fast as I can, and, sacking off a plain croissant, I order a homemade slice of Victoria sponge with fresh blueberry compote and cream cheese. I sit at a table in the corner, under ivy trailing from the window ledge, and leave on my sunglasses because I reckon I might cry again. Whatever made me sob in the Rookfield estate has set off a trail of tear-bombs in my head.

It begins to hit me that, in the space of twelve months, I've met and become firm friends with Sheila and have found out that I can hear and communicate with 'voices' because I'm clairaudient. I've realized that Frank, my dead friend, is still my mate and is still talking to me (when he can be arsed). I've nearly been killed by Creepy Dan the Creepy Murderer and had the stress of thinking he was going to kill Sheila as well and it would be my fault. I've met, had a fab affair with and then lost Pat, the sexy Irish barman. I've been haunted by Newcastle; seen my best friend possessed by a horrible ghost from a hundred years ago; met glorious Gladys, who was touched by tragedy herself and still sends me WhatsApp pictures of her new crystals; plus, last but not least, I met Caroline May, hated her, loved her and then she died. She not only died but phoned me after she was dead. And that was a matter of weeks ago. I'm grieving, I'm a bit traumatized, one of my best friends in London is moving to Scotland next week, I'm not sure I like the acting world any more and some-times, just sometimes, even though I love Inka, I'm extremely lonely.

I hate acknowledging the lonely bit, because I'm an

independent woman. I've always been an independent woman. But I'm sad sometimes that I've got no one. Except of course Neil the policeman, who has already enquired as to my plans tonight – I've been too busy getting haunted from every angle and escaping a terrible acting job to actually firm up a second date. As I lick cream cheese off my fork, I decide to dodge my feelings of grief and trauma by going to his later and banging him into next week. I'm pretty much positive that Caroline May would approve of this. Something seems to have changed in my 'well, at least try to pretend you're not a filthy cow' agenda. I need to crystallize all of these grief feelings into something positive. Tasty sex. I thoroughly understand that this is not healthy, and I suspect I'd be a Freudian's wet dream.

I text Neil, letting him know I'll be popping over by 6.30 p.m. I need to make the chilli first, as I try not to make promises I cannot keep.

BERRYISH KISS

Neil's flat is just as clean the second time, though the lilies are on the turn, which means the scent is going towards sickly. The smell reminds me of my dreams of old Southwark. Neil is delighted when he sees the casserole dish of food. The lad likes his scran. He's wearing a thick cotton T-shirt with a V-neck and I know how shallow it is, but the fine chest hair poking out is pretty crazy-making to me.

'Look, Tanz, I can't expect you to stay in again, so I've booked us a little booth at the place down the road, so I can treat you to some fizz.'

I'm not sure what I think about this, as I simply want to climb all over him on his massive sofa and forget every damn thing that's messing with my head, but it's very sweet that he wants to treat me as more than a booty call.

'Oh, what a treat! Should we eat when we get back or before?'

'Are you hungry yet?'

'Not massively.'

'Right, well, let me show you my favourite local, then afterwards maybe we can watch a movie of your choice with a big bowl of that tasty dish you've brought with you.'

He looks so pleased to see me. It's nice. Even though he seemed like a twelve-year-old to me when I first met him, it turns out he's kooky and clever and, now that we've been naked together, I know he's a bit of a caveman too. It's nice to be considered, as well as desired; he didn't have to book anything, but he's made the effort.

The booth, it turns out, is quirky and cool. It's more of a wine bar than a pub that he's brought me to, but it's cosy and he's booked us a little table for two with a crescent-shaped, brown fake-leather sofa around it. It's tucked away and quite private. Neil says he's happy to get us champagne, but I really fancy trying a cocktail. The list looks yummy. We have a hurricane lamp on the table, made of violet glass with a huge beeswax candle in it. It smells divine, though I reckon it's too big for the table space if you want to order plates of food. As it is, we both order a Berry Collins, which is lovely. The place is seemingly lit solely by these candles, plus dim little wall-lights.

Suddenly he blurts out: 'I think I hate my job. It might be time for a change.'

I am completely caught off guard by this comment.

'What? I know you said it's not quite how you expected, but I didn't think you were thinking of quitting!'

'You have no idea how boring St Albans is, crime-wise. It's all shitty misdemeanours and too much paperwork. The detective work is pretty mundane.'

'So, you really were hoping for more murders?'

'Of course I was.'

'It's funny, you know, the first time I met you, you looked pretty stoked to be a policeman and you were working bloody Traffic.'

'That was because someone else was off sick. I'm in the office as much as anything. Plus, something extraordinary had happened. I could hardly believe what I was hearing at first. All ghosts and knives and people locked in cupboards. That stuff doesn't happen around here. That's the stuff you want to hear about.'

'What will you do for money, if you're not a copper?'

'I've got a few ideas. I'm not thick, you know?'

'I know you're not.'

'I get the feeling you're used to blokes not being as smart as you are. I nearly am.'

I never think big-headed thoughts like that out loud. But it's true. I don't like ignorant people or those who have 'normal' thoughts, because I cannot be myself around them; plus, I do find that a lot of people don't think as quickly as I do. Not that it makes my decision-making any better. I still choose terrible men to commit to, and I still don't listen to my gut enough.

'Well, someone's been thinking some deep thoughts.'

'I think them all the time, and I think about you a lot as well. Your first impression of me was wrong. But I'm hoping I've brought you round, with my extra depths and irresistible charm.'

He pulls a ridiculous 'ugly' face and it sets me off. I lean in and give him a berryish kiss. As I'm pulling away, another body squashes into our little booth. A lass in a tight black dress with long, wavy brown hair sits on the other side of Neil and smacks her handbag and a pint on the table.

'Hello, Neil.' She sounds drunk. 'Who's your friend then?'

'Carla!'

Neil keeps his demeanour pleasant, but he doesn't sound pleased. I think it's a bit early to be drunk, frankly, but with my track record, who am I to judge?

Carla thrusts her hand across the table at me. 'I'm Carla.'

I shake it; it's warm and a bit too moist. 'I'm Tanz. Hello, Carla.'

'Oh, a northerner – a Geordie is it? Hello-o-o, Cheryl Cole.'

Wow, her banter stinks. Neil shakes his head at her. I surreptitiously wipe my hand on my skirt.

'What can I do for you, Carla? I can see your friends over there. They're probably wondering what you're up to.'

'I just fancied a change of scenery. How ya doing, Neil?'

'The same as I was doing at work today.'

'You look a bit more preoccupied now. Kissy-kissy face. Like when you were all kissy face with me.'

As soon as she says this, I decide I should grab my bag and drive home. Typical! It makes me feel sad that I can't have a fucking minute's nice time without some bullshit or other spoiling it. I can only imagine that Neil's a player who just got rumbled by his usual squeeze. Men are so fucking shitty. I go to stand up.

Neil puts his hand on mine, looks at me imploringly.

'Please, Tanz, don't. It's not what it looks like.'

'It's exac-c-ctly what it looks like!'

Carla takes a huge swig of her pint and grins at me. The glint in her eye is sharper than a paring knife. Her lips are wet with lager.

'We work in the same building, Tanz. Known each other ages. Love a bit of kissy face, we do. But he keeps bringing in these little slappers who don't get it.'

Neil's face drains of colour. He stands.

'If the sight of a beautiful, classy woman makes you this ugly, Carla, then I'd suggest that you maybe lay off the pints. You've done it now. Don't ever speak to me again. In the pub or at work. Do you understand?'

She screws up her face and grabs his arm.

'I was only messing! I was only messing, Neil. Come on, she's just a—'

While she's pulling at Neil's arm, Carla manages to upend the rest of her pint all over herself. She lets out a shriek and a mate of hers comes haring over, all massive gold hoops and big hair. To be fair, she looks quite fierce, in a good way. I like her orange dress with the orange nails.

'Carla, what the *fuck* are you doing?' She's drunk as well. They certainly start early round here.

Neil takes two notes out of his wallet and hands them to one of the staff to cover the cocktails, then holds out his hand to me. 'Let's go.'

I walk with him and, outside the pub, he leans against the wall, looking mortified.

'Please don't think I'm a wanker, Tanz. I'm sorry. We kissed at the Christmas party a year ago – both of us pissed – and she won't leave it.'

'You know, I always end up feeling like I did something wrong when it comes to other lasses. Why should I believe you're not a player?'

To be fair, Neil's doing a good job of looking crestfallen right now.

'I've dated a few women, it's true, but I'm single, it's allowed. And I don't cheat once I meet someone I like. I'm not a player. I simply don't want to "settle" for someone ordinary, and St Albans isn't exactly brimming with gorgeous northern witches. I like people who are different. I'm so sorry. I bet you want to go home now.' He sighs.

I grab him and kiss him. 'Beautiful' and 'classy', that's what he said about me. Plus, he wasn't a coward; he handled it. In those circumstances it wasn't my place to defend myself, and I didn't have to; it was his shit and he dealt with it without getting aggressive or nasty. Some blokes wouldn't know what to do, but he did. I just want to get back to his place as quickly as possible and lose myself in sex. I've had enough drama over the past year, but I like Neil's style right now and I shall cut him some slack.

He pulls his head back and looks at me.

'You are the most surprising woman I've ever come across. Can we go to mine and pretend I didn't take you to a bar with a nutty stalker in it?'

'Okay, but you're on probation. That was excruciating.'

'Fair enough. I'll try to make it up to you, I promise.'

I'm already looking forward to him making it up to me. For the rest of the night.

ANGEL OF THE NORTH

Sheila and I thought coming out on a Sunday night was the best idea, as the world is much quieter on Sunday nights. What we didn't consider was quite how bloody freezing it would be after midnight. It's been mild recently, but I didn't figure on the lateness or the closeness to the river. I've driven us to Cross Bones and getting out of the car is quite a shock, as the temperature has plummeted. We both button our coats to the top.

Louisa is standing at the gate, holding a torch. As we approach, she hands us both a big woollen shawl each. According to the light from her torch, they are glorious colours.

'Oh my goodness, these are lovely!' Sheila's looks like it's purple and turquoise.

Louisa grins at her.

'I love to knit. These are yours to keep. I realized when I stepped out of the house that it was a bit nippy, so I grabbed you one each.'

The torch catches bright pink and mustard-yellow on

mine. I can't work out the other flecks of colour, but I adore it. And wrapped around my head and draped over my shoulders, it's toasty.

'Louisa, these are brilliant.'

She winks. 'Always be prepared!'

She has already unlocked the gate and locks it behind us as we make our way into the graveyard. Both Sheila and I have our little torches on now. I ordered these mini torches with really strong bulbs on them. The beam is surprisingly wide and very bright.

We go through the entrance 'tunnel' bit, which has a wooden roof built over it, then emerge via a little peaked wooden roof into the graveyard proper. Louisa picks up a folding seat and points to two more.

'This way we can sit anywhere you think is appropriate.'

She's really thought this through. Sheila picks up hers, then sniffs the air.

'Can you smell that?' She looks at me.

'That's an industrial smell, that. And death.'

There is a rotten smell for sure. Sweet and on the turn, like Neil's lilies, but not flowers – meat. Also, soot and smoke. Louisa shines her torch around the graveyard and on the ground in a ten-foot circle.

'I can't smell what you're smelling, and there's nothing rotting around here. Just so you know.'

I let Sheila go in front of me, while Louisa walks behind. Sheila will know where to put the chairs down. She's a fucking genius when it comes to ghostly stuff; she tunes in so succinctly, from years of experience basically. She halts before we get to the whitewashed wall at the other end. (It has writing on it and a poem about the Winchester Geese, a bit further along.) She puts down her seat, facing into the graveyard, and we follow suit, with me next to Sheila, and Louisa next to me.

'Right, girls, I think we need to put our torches away and hold hands. Whatever's going on, I'm only here to amplify Tanz's perception. It's her gig, I can feel it.'

I look at her. 'Are you sure?'

'Definitely. The graveyard wants you here. It has something to tell you.'

I get a chill up my spine. Part excitement, part fear. I'm still comparatively new to this stuff. *What does this graveyard want with me?*

We all hold hands and close our eyes. Well, I think we do, because I can't see the other two, but I definitely close mine. Without the torches it's quite an exhilarating thing, sitting here in the cold and dark. Luckily the flats across the road still have some lights on and there are lamp posts out there, so it's not quite black as pitch in here, but it's pretty bleedin' dark. The hands of the other two are warm and it provides some comfort.

Sheila speaks. 'Okay, Tanz, this is your call. We'll stay quiet until you've seen or heard what you need to.'

I'm feeling a bit queer. It's like there are suddenly people around us everywhere, pressing in. I grip the lasses' hands more tightly and now, in my mind's eye, it's not night. It's day and there's a burial going on. There are five coffins: four adult-sized and one tiny. They're all to be placed in one hole. The stink is disgraceful. There's a small, shrivelled vicar reading some kind of service. The people attending look almost as dead as whoever they're burying.

Then I see Oonah, the woman I spoke to in that room filled with the starving Irish family. She is holding the hand of a tiny girl who must be about three, and the tears are rolling down her face as the little girl stands wide-eyed and uncomprehending. I realize that I'm watching the burial of everyone else who'd been in that room. Only Oonah and the little girl survived. I wonder where the hell the stench is coming from, then see an opening with stairs down, under grass level. There's a grille opening out onto the graveyard. I'm pretty sure this must be the bone-house that I've read about, full of decomposing bodies and the mulch of not-totally-rotted flesh on the floor.

The graveyard is surrounded by houses, their windows within feet of all this action, and I can see the school too. This means it must be later, closer to the date when the graveyard closed. I wouldn't want to be the people who overlooked this place. I get closer to Oonah and it looks like she might faint. She's so sunken and so upset. And the little girl, sweetly innocent. I can't bear it. I rack my brains to think how to help. I remember the old lady in the rocking chair across the road, now a street behind the houses overlooking the graveyard. I wonder if she was from the same time. I take a deep breath and visualize her.

Suddenly I'm outside a small house with a bright-red door. Then I'm inside and the fire is roaring. Kath, the eccentric knitter, is there. She's wearing her woollen cap and talking away to herself. I'm not sure how to approach her or whether she'll hear me.

'Kath. KATH! There's something you need to do.'

Kath stops rocking and looks around her.

'Who's there? Are you the devil?'

'Erm, no . . . No, I'm an angel, and you have a mission.'

'Well, that's an 'orrible way of talkin', for an angel.'

Wow, people usually like my accent. I soften my voice.

'Kath. A young woman came over from Ireland, from the famine. All her family just died, except one little wee one. They're starving. Could you spare the tiniest bit of food? Only a tiny bit?'

Kath looks put out.

'I'm not a toff, you know – not got food comin' out me ears. And those Irish . . . take the shirt off your back.'

Bloody hell, she sounds like my mam. I look around. Kath's not rich, but she has a good fire, little knick-knacks. She has someone looking after her. I feel it's a son. She's doing better than most.

'These are good people. You'll secure your place in heaven just for a bite to eat for a good girl and a tiny child.'

Kath thinks, then shrugs.

'Send 'em 'ere then, I don't go out there. I've got mutton and a bit o' bread I baked. And a little bit o' cheese. I can wrap it up in paper for 'em. I don't like visitors, so they can't stay.'

'You're a good, good woman. Thank you, Kath. Watch out your window for them . . .'

'I'll wrap 'em now and wait at the door. Hand it over an' that's that.'

The funeral rites have been performed and the coffins

are being piled into the ground. It's a pathetic sight. Oonah, obviously feeling sick and in deep grief, has backed off and is near the entrance. The little girl, hit by the strangeness of everything, has begun to cry. I can't bear the look of helplessness on Oonah's face. I reckon she's younger than I first assumed. She's so thin and dirty, it was hard to tell. I decide it's time to speak to her.

'Oonah.'

Her head lifts, she looks around.

'Who's there?'

'I'm your friend, Oonah.'

The little girl looks up. I assume she's Oonah's niece. She obviously wants to know who her aunt just spoke to.

'Oonah, there's a door across the road. It's bright red. Knock – knock and the lady there will help you.'

Oonah wipes the tears from her face with the back of her hand. When she speaks, it's in a whisper.

'I can't. They don't like the Irish around here.'

'Oonah, do it. You have nothing to lose. The little one needs food. Knock on the door and you'll get a tiny bit of help.'

'Who are you?'

'I'm a friend. I wish I could help more. I'll be with you when you knock. Please.'

Oonah looks down at the little girl, who has a sore on her lip, but has the most heart-melting pale-green eyes.

'Come on, Brid, we've got an errand to do.'

They exit the graveyard, and the red door is unmissable across the road. I whisper encouragement.

'I'm with you . . .'

She takes a breath, and they cross. They reach the door. Oonah looks so nervous, she steps back and tells Brid to knock.

Kath, looking pretty fearsome in the face and clutching a small brown-paper package, opens the door and finds herself looking down into the eyes of this tiny mite.

Brid speaks up. Her voice is a funny squeak.

'*Hello. I like your door.*'

Kath's demeanour changes immediately. She laughs widely at the little girl, baring the few teeth she has left.

'*Well, look at you, you little darlin'. No wonder you've got a guardian angel.*'

She looks at Oonah, who is standing a few paces away, and sees a young woman about to collapse.

'*Hey, sit down on the wall. Don't be fallin' into a faint on the front path. Well, ain't you the tiny sliver of a thing. Wait there – here you go, young lady, you take care of that.*'

She hands Brid the package, but Brid is too shy to open it. Kath returns with a tin cup and hands it to Oonah.

'*Drink this – good ale that, it'll sort out the faints.*'

She then produces from her apron pocket what looks like some kind of cake. She hands a slice of it to Brid, who takes a bite, and her eyes widen at Kath.

'*This is lovely, Missus.*'

Kath laughs and hands another slice to Oonah.

'*Clever girl there. Saving the package 'til she gets 'ome. Not a greedy one, 'er, a proper little doll. I baked this myself, little dolly!*'

Oonah begins to cry again.

'*Thank you so much. I don't know how to pay you back.*'

Kath's eyes narrow. Not one to miss a trick, this one.

'*Come back same time next week and do my washing. I hate the washing. I'll give you food again. Bring the little 'un. She reminds me of my Archie when he was tiny. Built like a carthorse now. And don't bring anyone else. I ain't a charity house.*'

Before I can see any more, I'm back in the cemetery. There's no funeral happening now. It's twilight and I see children and adults, crying, screaming, coughing and laughing. People of all different ages, judging by their clothes. They're transparent but there, reliving their last moments, or the moments they held dearest. I don't know why I'm seeing all of this. Prostitutes with well-dressed men, beggars covered in sores, ragged workers with sunken eyes and deep coughs, measles spots on babies in cots and vomiting old ladies lying in the hay. Kisses and cries and laughs and sobs. It's overwhelming and I need it to stop, as I'm choking with the intensity of it all. And then . . . for one tiny second, I see her. Finally. A vision of the girl with red hair from Charlie's photograph. Jill. She's holding what looks like a mug of coffee, sitting at a small modern-ish dining table and laughing her head off at something.

After one flash of her face, I hear a crashing noise and suddenly Sheila lets go of my hand and I blink my eyes open. Louisa switches on her torch.

'The wall!'

The walkway into the cemetery has a drystone wall on one side, obviously built by hand. And now one section of it is on the ground. Louisa sighs.

'Oh dear. Would anyone like a peppermint tea? I've

brought a big flask. Should we get warmed up in my car and have a chat about what just happened? I'm going to have to explain this to Heather tomorrow. She will not be pleased.'

The thought of hot tea is a welcome one. I'm shaking with emotion and my nose is icy. That was a lot.

EXTRA BATTERY INDEED

Louisa's car is a big old-fashioned Volvo estate and I really like it. We're not all cramped up. I sit in the back while she runs the engine for two minutes with the heating on full, and nurse a cup that she hands me filled with hot peppermint tea. A few sips and I start feeling better. Sheila sits in the front and nestles into her woollen shawl as she receives her own cup. Another minute and Louisa turns off the engine.

'Don't want to leave it on too long. Not very eco-friendly.' We nod in agreement. Louisa grimaces. 'That was intense. Much more of this and the whole place is going to fall down around our ears. Heather's going to have a fit.'

'Tanz here is going to find the key to stopping it, aren't you?'

'Oh, thanks, Sheils – no pressure then.'

Louisa looks impressed.

'So, girls, you do this kind of thing quite a lot, I'm guessing?'

Sheila nods. 'Mostly me though, love. Tanz is scared of ghosts.'

'Cheeky mare. I just had to watch the whole bloody cemetery light up with people. I thought I was going to be sick. Did you see anything, Louisa? You were very quiet. I'd expect a civilian to get a bit scared.'

She looks at us both excitedly.

'I closed my eyes, like Sheila said to, and at first I simply "felt" that it wasn't only us three. I squinted one eye open because I got a bit alarmed and, well, I saw something . . .'

'Oh, well done for not screaming, love.'

Louisa grins at Sheila when she says this.

'I've always felt there was more to the world than what meets the eye, but until you two showed up at the grave-yard I'd never seen anything out of the ordinary myself. Then I saw that old gravedigger and I wasn't as scared as I thought I'd be. I knew that he couldn't see me, and he was nothing to be afraid of. Just then, when I opened my one eye, there was a soldier! He can't have been from this graveyard, because he was in a Second World War uniform and this place closed more than eighty years before that broke out. He was standing there looking confused, like he didn't know where he was. He had a nice face. Sad, though. Blood on his head – I think he was shot. I wasn't scared at all. I wanted to comfort him, but didn't know how.'

'Bloody hell, that's quite a thing to see without being scared. You're braver than me, and I'm a Geordie! How weird, though. I saw nothing to do with soldiers. What did he look like?'

Louisa sips her tea as she thinks.

'He had warm eyes, even though he looked sad. About thirty and really seemed like he didn't know what was going on. Perhaps, when he was killed, it was such a shock he didn't realize at first that he was dead. He seemed to be searching for someone, turning his head about.'

'Well observed, love!' Sheila looks at me, thoughtful. 'What did you see, Tanz? I thought you were going to crush the bones in my hand at one point.'

I explain about Oonah and Brid, the little one, plus the lady across the road who knits. Then I tell them about seeing so many layers of the dead, all making a cacophonous racket at the same time, and how it nearly made me sick it was so overwhelming. For some reason, I miss out the blink-and-you'll-miss-it vision of Jill at the end. That seemed to be unattached to the rest of it, and I need to work out why on earth she popped up. When I finish, both women look quite gobsmacked by my adventure. Sheila's not saying much. I wonder what she's thinking?

'What about you, Sheila, what did you see?'

'I was your extra battery, remember, so I didn't see as much as you two. And I have to say, Louisa, you look very tired after your adventure. Thank you for the tea, but I really think you should be driving home to bed now.'

Louisa doesn't disagree and stifles a yawn with her hand.

'I'm so sorry, girls. This is really interesting, but I was up early this morning and I'm getting up before seven tomorrow.'

'Don't be daft. Thanks for letting us visit at such an inconvenient time.' I hand her my cup.

Sheila pours the last of hers out of the window, then also hands it over.

'Sorry, Louisa, if I had the lot, I'd wet myself on the way home.'

I realize that this is probably going to happen to me, after drinking most of mine, but it's too late now. We bid her good night, then get into my little tin can on wheels. I start it up and wang the heating on full straight away. As we're pulling round the corner, onto the first road towards north London, I see blanket-man. He's stumbling along, blanket on his head and another around his shoulders, carrying a large bottle of cider and shouting. I can't hear what he's saying, but he doesn't look happy. In fact, he looks haunted. Sometimes I wonder if that's how I'll end up, if I don't ease up on the booze. I flick a quizzical glance at Sheila as we leave him behind.

'What the hell was that about – you being my extra battery and all that shit? When did you *ever* see less than me, you bloody fibber?'

She laughs. 'I need to talk to you, tell you some things. Thought it was better if we were already driving home. They don't concern Louisa.'

'Oh?'

'You do realize what you just did, don't you? I've never heard the like of it.'

'What do you mean?'

'We see them, we talk to them, we ask why they're still around, we try to help them on, while they're stuck, right?'

'Yes, right.'

'What we don't do – and what I've never managed to do

in my whole bloody life – is talk to the dead in their life-times and negotiate them a food parcel . . .' She begins to cackle, and I end up joining in. Put like that, it's preposterous.

'So, this has never happened to you?'

'Of course it's never happened to me. I'm a bloody medium, not a fairy godmother. Someone is guiding you into helping those from the past. And someone – I don't know if it's the same person – is lighting up the lives and deaths of those who passed in the area. Tuning into them, tuning you into them, guiding you to be their guide. There's a pattern here. The Irish accents, the woman in the rocking chair . . . What else? The gravedigger, the woman you saw nursing her husband. I don't know who else you've been dropping in on. But someone, or something, has made you far more receptive. *Far more*, so that you're tuning in left, right and centre. Hence suddenly seeing the nurse in your flat, who's probably been pootling about since you moved in. You just didn't see her until you were activated.'

'Wait a minute! Frank said I'd been "activated". Then fucked off without an explanation. I wonder if it's got anything to do with that soft-voiced lass who pops up in my head and explains what's going on with the Southwark spooks. She's never told me her name.'

Sheila does one of her little whistles.

'Thing is, Tanz, I did see something. I wanted to hear your story first, to see if it made any sense. But you have so much going on – this is a lot to put on you spiritually. Like a test. I could see all kinds of people around the graveyard. I could feel and hear the gravedigger, and I know why you saw him and why he's still around. He was old and tired, and the parish was paying him to dig bodies back up, hardly rotted half the time, and take them to the bone-house and chop them up with his shovel. It looked like he and the other gravediggers were disrespectful to the bodies and had become quite immune to what they were doing.

'But one time in particular, not long before his death, a teenage boy was dug back up. A boy who had been buried in a blue shift. It was an unusual and recognizable shirt, and the gravedigger was considering having it off him before he was buried. The skull came away from the body just as a young lady came into the grounds. I think that young lady was your Oonah, and she ran in and screamed at the old fella. It was her brother. Her devastation really affected him, like no one else's ever had. He died feeling very guilty. That's why you're feeling him. Your hauntings are all connected to Oonah somehow. I tried to reach out to her, but it's only you who can actually speak to her. She's locked in the trauma of her life. I can't tell you what happened next, but let's say things don't exactly get better for her.'

'Oh no. And what about Brid?'

'Who knows? I couldn't even see her. But I did link into your Kath. Funny old bird, wasn't she? Not as hard as she tried to seem. She knitted the little one a shawl and socks, I think. I saw her making them. She really liked the little girl.'

'Well, that's something.'

'Yes, that's something. And it looks like a network of

people has been highlighted by someone with a very strong psychic light. They're extremely powerful. Seemingly, this in turn has managed to light up and highlight the lives of lots of unrelated dead folk who are buried here. I don't think that's intentional, but it has to stop. The place is falling down from the force of the energy. I've never seen anything like it!'

Sheila stops and peers at me. 'Tanz. Are you okay, love?'

'Yeah, I'm fine, thanks. Just bursting for the loo.'

She laughs. 'Stop at the garage. You can sort yourself out and we can get some chocolate. We've earned it.'

She's right. I'm flagging a bit, and a cheeky treat will do the trick. We stop and, on top of the immense relief of an empty bladder, I get the treat of a sugar-rush.

It keeps gnawing at me that nothing is ever clear-cut or simple. I always have to work things out, like I'm in *The Crystal Maze*. And this time the clues aren't leading me anywhere fast and it's getting on my tits.

'I know you're listening, Frank. I'm not going back and forth to Southwark indefinitely, you twat. Plus, what was that sudden snapshot of Jill, after absolutely nothing?'

No answer. Typical. Then the soft-voiced lass is here. While Sheila sucks on her Double Decker, I hear her clearly.

'*I'm so sorry, Tanz. This is such a jumble.*'

'Hello, you. I wish you'd give me a name. I keep calling you "soft-voiced lass".'

'*That's as good a name as any. Right now, we must sort out this thing with the graveyard . . . She's called Nelly.*'

'Who?'

'*She's in a pickle. She's like you, a true psychic, but she's never really known what to do with it. And now she's dying, and she needs to speak to you. She doesn't mean to illuminate everything like this. She's picking through the past and hardly knows what she's doing. If I help you find her, you should be able to sort this out. I'm afraid I didn't help her at all.*'

'You know you've just made this sound even more complicated? Why can't anyone simply tell me what's going on? So you already tried to help Nelly and couldn't? Does this mean I have to go back to Southwark this week?'

'*If you don't mind?*'

'I do bloody mind.'

Sheila looks at me with chocolate smeared on her top lip.

'Tanz, what's wrong? You've got a face like a slapped arse.'

'Soft voiced-lass is here, and she says I have to go back again this week. I'm a north London dweller, Sheils, this is really doing my head in now.'

Sheila sucks chocolate off her thumb and winks at me.

'They don't listen to reason. They tell you what needs to be done. It's up to you whether you react. But if you don't, it usually gets trickier.'

'Oh, for fuck's sake, what do you mean by "trickier"?'

Sheila chortles.

'Well, better that you do what they ask than they start parading solid ghosts through your bedroom.'

'They'd better bloody not!'

I hear soft-voiced lass as I try to close my mind down.
I'm so bloody tired.

'I wouldn't do that to you. Promise.'
I don't know whether to believe her.

LOVELY GLADYS

I thought I'd fall asleep immediately, but I'm too jumpy. So much going on, and still no proper answers. I keep thinking I'm going to see a ghost again and I can't help feeling sad for all those souls in that little graveyard. They were people with hopes and dreams, they all mattered and yet nobody seemed to care in those days. It was brutal.

The phone rings, which is quite a shock as I thought I'd put it on silent. Plus, it's ridiculous-o'clock. I check and it's Gladys! Cake-loving, super-psychic, funny, lovely Gladys from Newcastle. Why is she calling me in the middle of the night?

'Hello?'

'Tanz, how are you, me little Viennese whirl?'

'I'm okay. Are you all right, Gladys? It's three a.m., you know!'

'Oh, I know, I woke up fancyin' a cup of tea and a biscuit. I sleep like a medieval monk, me. Earlyish to bed 'til about now. Then three more hours' sleep after I've had me tea and a chat with me crystals. I like it.'

'Well, I'm usually conked out at this time, so you're lucky to get me.'

'I had a little message from one of them upstairs, sayin' you weren't asleep. She's an angel. I call her Rhiannon, after one of my favourite songs. It's not her real name, but she likes it.'

I fucking love Gladys.

'She was tellin' me it's all been kickin' off for you and that you might need a little boost. I need your address off you, because I want to send you a crystal that'll help. But also I wanted to check if you're all right.'

'I'm fine, just a bit confused by what's going on. I don't understand the higgledy-piggledy way the spirits are behaving. It's all mysterious clues. Either they need my assistance, or they don't. But they simply seem to be messing with me.'

'Right. I need to tell you somethin'. Do you want to get a cuppa for yourself?'

'I've got a ginger tea right here, Gladys, thought it might calm my brain down.'

'That's good. You see you were prepared; you knew I would call! Now here's what's happenin', as far as Rhiannon says.'

Because she's called Rhiannon, I can't help seeing Gladys's angel as Stevie Nicks. It's perfect.

'You know when someone dies that you care about, it can open all kinds of psychic portals?'

'Sort of . . .'

'It's like your talent for connectin' goes through the roof, because there's less of a barrier between you and the next world, or plane, or whatever you believe in.'

'Right . . .'

'So when your Caroline May died, it tuned you in higher, right, like suddenly your wobbly telly picture was as clear as a bell. It meant that if someone was tryin' to get a message through to you, they could do it easily. It was most powerful just as she died. All these doors opened up so much that she could speak to you through the phone and you really thought she'd called you, she was so clear.'

'Yes. That's true.'

This brings a lump to my throat. I hope Caroline is okay now. I've not heard anything from her since.

'Now you're visitin' a new place in that London. You're visitin' somewhere, aye?'

'Yes, Cross Bones Graveyard in Southwark.'

'Oooh, the Winchester Geese.'

'Bloody hell, am I the only one who hadn't heard of them?'

She chuckles.

'I do a lot of readin', me. So, you're visiting this grave-yard. What took you there?'

I explain about Charlie and his sister Jill, who defo didn't die on that street; and how as soon as I arrived on Union Street I was 'sucked down the road'; and how there are apparitions and imprints bloody everywhere.

'Now that's clever. Because that initial visit took you to your true purpose and, accordin' to Rhiannon, who's chewin' me ear off here . . . All right, Rhiannon, can you slow down, please? Sorry, Tanz. The person you're lookin' for lives in the same block that Jill's boyfriend lived in. She even met Jill. That's the connection, I reckon. Now this lady you're lookin' for has not got long left to live, but she's bloody powerful. Like a beacon. Because she's close to the next "plane", she's openin' doors up left, right and centre, throwin' light on the dead and reignitin' lost memories. They're so full-on, people who are only a little bit psychic are also seein' things that they usually wouldn't see and wouldn't want to. She's lookin' for something or someone, and you're the only one who can sort this. Find her and you find the source. Her name's Nelly. She worked with disadvantaged kids for years; she's a good, good woman. Look for her . . .'

'Oh my goodness, Gladys, that's brilliant. I have this new voice in my head – she hasn't told me her name and I just call her "soft-voiced lass." She told me there was a "Nelly".'

'Yes, I got a feelin' about another lass who's helping. She's got a secret. I can't feel what it is, either. But don't worry, your Frank wouldn't have brought her to you if she was dangerous.'

'How did you know Frank brought her?'

'Told you, Rhiannon won't stop blinkin' talkin'. She's very excited. She says if you lie down, she'll give you a healin' so you sleep well, and your mind strengthens. You've got some decisions to make.'

'I know I have.'

'Mebbes we can chat again when it's not the middle of the night. Not that I mind, but other people seem to! Text me your address, please.'

'I will. And thank you, Gladys, I don't know what I'd do without my spooky friends.'

'Well, lie down now, pet, and Rhiannon'll sort you out. She's on a mission. I reckon I'll get myself a slice of Battenberg, then I'll hit the hay as well.'

'Okay. Love you, Gladys.'

'Love you too, pet.'

Within minutes I'm lying on my back, with only the light from the hallway casting a glow on the far wall. I feel a pressure on my shoulders and chest, and suddenly my head empties of cares and worries and fills instead with the heat of a late-afternoon sun. It's lovely. I feel my whole body go limp. Deep inside my suddenly relaxed mind, I whisper, 'Thank you, Rhiannon.'

The reply is also whispered.

'Enjoy your power. Always enjoy . . .'

I don't hear anything else as I fall into a deep sleep.

THE BIG SLEEP

How have I woken up at noon? Lucky there was still dry food in the bowl for Inka or she'd have mauled my face off by now. *It's noon!*

Whatever Rhiannon did, it's really sorted me out. My shoulders had been creeping up my neck due to anxiety the past few days, and I've been sleeping in fits and starts. Now I've slept for eight or nine hours on the trot and nothing aches. This is stupendous.

I jump up, put on my satin dressing gown and run to the loo, as I've not been for *hours*. Once Inka has fresh food and I have a coffee, I go to my comfy armchair and let the sun shine on me through the open blinds. Those feelings that have been coursing through me: grief, sadness, worry about the future, a feeling of doom, of time passing too quickly, of being trapped in the wrong life. It hits me properly now – they're not my feelings. Some of them are, but they've been exacerbated. They've been magnified by the strong feelings of the people I've been tuning into, and who have been tuning into me, so I need to separate them all out, like a logic problem. That's how I'll deal with this. I've not been protecting myself enough, it turns out. I've not taken seriously enough how much 'tuning in' can damage my psyche when I don't separate the feelings of others from my own. I need stronger protection and a 'sensible' approach to the spooky stuff.

'*Somebody's growing up.*'

'Shut it, Frank.'

'*Charming.*'

'Where've you been?'

'*Doing cool stuff.*'

'I got a healing from Rhiannon. It was so lovely; I still feel stoned.'

'*That's what it feels like when you stop stressing for a minute.*'

'To be fair, it's not all my stress. Ghosts, and new voices in my head and all sorts. Most of that is your fault.'

'*It's your fault. I didn't make you into a witch. But it's true, you need to protect yourself. Rhiannon wants to help. Call on her and ask her to give you the right protection, so you can separate yourself from the intense thoughts of those you're tapping into. She helped you last night, so she's still probably close.*'

'Okay, thanks.'

'*I can't say I approve of you having another new boyfriend, by the way. But at least this one shares your gruesome fascination with horrible murderers.*'

'Number one, he's not my boyfriend; and number two, you weren't exactly innocent when it came to my entanglement with a very recent gruesome murderer, if I remember rightly.'

'*You're dying to see him again, Tanz, he's definitely your boyfriend. And by the way, don't forget Tom today.*'

'Wha—OH, FUCK!'

I'm having a coffee with Tom from the Old Red Lion in an hour – I forgot all about it. If I drive and park in the car park behind the shopping centre I'll be on time, but I'll have to leave very soon. I leg it to the shower.

PLAY TIME

Obviously I'm in a devil-may-care mood today, as I've driven all the way to where Gerald Birch lives. No mean feat across London by day. But he says he has a great builders' caff near him that serves all-day breakfast, and evidently that is our thing now. I didn't want to go to his house, as I know his wife's in and she wants him out from under her feet – not a crackers actress showing up and adding to the general feeling of overcrowdedness.

He's sitting in the window of the caff with a book and a huge mug of tea. He waves expansively as I approach. Gerald has the most gloriously big and expressive face. How could he be anything but an actor? He stands up when I reach him and does the each-cheek air-kiss.

'Well, hello, my darling. Couldn't keep away from me, obviously!'

'Well, *obviously*, Gerald.'

An older lady in a pinny with dry hair-ends and long roots comes over with a little notepad and stub of a pencil. Gerald nods to her.

'I didn't order this time, in case you wanted something different.'

'You did right. I've been eating far too much recently, so today I'm having a mushroom omelette and an Americano with oat milk on the side, please.'

'Well, I'm not eating like a child for anyone, and I would like the full works, please! White toast.'

The lady winks at Gerald, who's obviously a regular. And then he puts his palms down on the table and regards me.

'So-o-o, what brings you to the East End, young lady? Do you have tidings?'

'I do. I had a chat with Tom at the Old Red Lion today. Talked to him about a comedy play that my best friend Milo wrote. It's the same length as that piece of shit we were just rehearsing, but this one is actually witty and worth watching. According to Tom, there's a gap in the timetable at the minute. There was our show, then two weeks with nothing booked, then another show starts: a review of some kind. If we start in a week, we'll still have the two-week rehearsal time. He said – and you mustn't tell anyone this, because it's not usual – that he's still got the theatre hire fee from Maeve; she couldn't simply pull out like that, so she lost the money. Therefore, it won't hurt Tom to put on our show two weeks late, for a week. We can even split the door profit as extra pay, on top of the free wages we already got. It might only be a few quid in the end, but we *have* already been paid for a job we didn't do. And I wouldn't have to invest anything in hiring the place, which would be perfect, as I have no spare cash to invest.

'What I want is to direct the play and have you three in the show. Milo's willing to do a tweak to make the characters work with you lot as the leads, but I'll only do it if you fancy it, Gerald. It's a three-hander and I don't care about being in it. I've got a couple of pals who work in props and so on, who'll be happy to help, and Tom's hired a techie for the next show, who wants to practise on the new sound and lighting board. So we'd have the lighting and sound covered. What do you think? You can read the play first, of course.'

'My dear girl, unless it's the worst play ever written since time began, wild horses couldn't stop me! I'd love to have you telling me what to do for a fortnight.'

'Ha, I don't think you'll take much telling, really. I suspect this might be right up your street.'

'Well, that's marvellous, and my wife is going to be cock-a-hoop. She'll now have the house to herself again for her coffee afternoons and her cackling circle of book-analysing wine-quaffers, who swear they're there for the intellectual debate and not the Chablis.'

Our food arrives and Gerald chuckles when he sees my plate. Evidently the omelette comes with an enormous pile of French fries. My mouth falls open, but I can't lie: a bit of me is delighted by this mountain of oily carbs. Before I can touch a single one, Gerald reaches forward like he's going to take my plate.

'Now, now, Tanz. You can't have them – you only wanted an omelette.'

I smack his hand with the wooden spoon that stands upright in a little jar with the table number on it.

'No, you don't. I know what I said, but if this omelette comes with chips, then I'm obliged to eat chips. My diet can start tomorrow.'

Gerald butters his toast and grins.

'That's more like it. Never did like fussy girls – no fun to eat out with. Always putting things to one side of the plate and turning their noses up. And always want "just one bite" of your dessert.'

'I've never stopped at one bite of dessert in my life.'

'Neither have they, the little shits.'

I think we'll do great things together on Milo's play. I just hope the other two are up for it. This is the first time I've been excited about work in a long time. What a relief to have something to look forward to, though I'm also nervous. Now I have to tell my agent.

ROBERT-THE-RAVISHING

Sleep came so easily to me tonight. I should have known I'd wake up in another place, this time in a bloody bombsite. And when I say 'bloody', people have died here. I know that as soon as I look around. There are bloodstains and I can feel the shock of the suddenly departed. A whole street has been mangled and destroyed. I'm standing on a pile of wood that could have been furniture at some point. There is no ceiling, just a few wonky beams and the grey-blue sky. The air smells of fire. There are children playing in the wreckage, and men in tin hats are ordering people to be careful. I can't help wondering where the survivors of this mess are going to live now.

There's a woman sitting on one remaining debris-covered chair about ten feet from me, in what seems to be a bombed-out living room. A wrecked piano nearby is baring its keys at the world, like comedy teeth. The woman looks to be around thirty. Pretty face, pale eyes and so much sorrow. She is utterly defeated. It's not simply the fact that her home has been bombed; it's more than that. She's lost someone recently. I can feel it vibrating from her.

I step closer and, as she cries, I feel her decision. She's going to end her life. She feels there's nothing left here. Her husband also died this week. He was away in the war. They didn't have children yet. She doesn't see the point of life any more.

Soft-voiced lass turns up.

'*Arnott Street in Southwark, 1940. It was the sixth of September – the day before her birthday.*'

'What can I do?'

'*Give her love.*'

I protect myself, ask Rhiannon, the Fleetwood Mac angel, to help me separate myself from the horror and grief, and then I concentrate every bit of healing energy I have on this poor lass. I imagine it enveloping her in warm light. I don't know who she is, so I concentrate on mentally stroking her, and whisper the first thing that comes into my head.

'You still have so much to do. You are going to help so many. And when you're done, he'll be waiting as if only a minute has passed.'

I literally have no idea where that came from; it just felt like the right thing to say. And I see this woman close her eyes as the tears fall even harder. I speak again because I cannot bear her sadness.

'You are so loved. You will always be loved. And you staying alive matters so very much.'

I feel this with every fibre. There's something about her that is incredible. I can suddenly see a light emanating from her, pinkish and utterly kind. Her aloneness makes me so sad. I know all about feeling alone, but I'm an amateur compared to her. She carries sadness from those who came before her in her family line, too. It seeps out of her: the saddest family history. And now this – everything gone. But it's not. She has strength like no one would believe; she merely needs a touch of hope.

'You will feel happiness again, I promise. And you will see him again. Love him in your heart 'til then.'

This is when she surprises me by speaking out loud.

'How can I believe that? How can I believe I'll see him? I can't take any more.'

I think about Gladys telling me about everything in the past few weeks being linked. I think about being in the graveyard the other night, and what Louisa saw. I take a punt, as it doesn't take a genius to work out that the soldier Louisa was talking about may have been this one's husband, the lost soul with a shot to the head. He'd have transitioned to the next world as soon as he orientated himself, so now, in this place between two times, I call on him. As I do so, I put my hand on this weeping woman's shoulder, hoping against hope that she feels something. To my relief, I sense another presence arrive. A man's.

'*Hello. Robert-the-ravishing here, reporting for duty.*'

His voice is friendly and he's taking the mick, which surprises me, but also makes things less formal.

'Robert, is this your wife?'

His voice is all warmth when he replies.

'*My Nelly, love of my life.*'

Nelly? Oh, wow. Now I get it.

'Well, you need to speak to her; she needs to know you'll look after her, and be with her, until her time on Earth is done. She must be convinced that she still has things to do, and a life to live!'

'*Oh, that's true, all right. I've never seen anyone stronger or more magical than my Nelly.*'

The pride in his voice burns brightly. I feel his energy move to her side, by her right ear, and I step back. I see Nelly's eyes widen and hear her gasp.

'Robert?'

I don't hear what he says to her, and I'm glad not to intrude on a husband and wife's private love and grief. As I see Nelly's face crumple, my own presence wanes. In the blink of an eye, I go from standing in a ruined street in Southwark to lying in my bed in Crouch End, tears leaking, grief-stricken wails coming from my surprised mouth. Protected or not, linking into her loneliness has knifed me in the heart.

So that was Nelly? If so, she'll now be well over a hundred years old. Really old, like one-of-the-oldest-people-in-the-country old. And even as I cry, I remember the woman who touched my arm the first time I went to Cross Bones. She looked like the oldest person I'd ever seen in my life, dressed up all smart with those pale, wise eyes. She seemed very much in the know about the graveyard. I can't help wondering if that's who I'm looking for. And if so, isn't it incredible that she found me first, even if she didn't know it?

WISE ELSA

I'm feeling pretty fucking odd as I walk down to Crouch End for a lunch date with Elsa. I mean, one minute I'm happy and laughing with Gerald, the next I'm stuck in a bombed street trying to persuade a lovely young woman who's lost everything not to kill herself. Plus, I keep getting tearful when I think of her husband, so pointlessly dead before they'd even had a chance to enjoy their lives together. How easy we all have it these days.

Still, however I'm feeling, I'd better pull myself together, as I think Elsa has enough on her plate right now. She's packed and ready, or so she says, but if I know Elsa at all, she's packed half of her flat and expects to pack the other half and get the whole place clean in a forty-eight-hour period, after taking a fortnight to do the first bit. She'll probably put out a distress call soon and expect all her friends to mobilize, and pack and clean, while she sits back and delegates. I have a gift with me, wrapped and ready, in case it's the last time I see her before she goes north, which is a distinct possibility, if she's not as prepared as she says she is. I've bought Elsa an antique silver bracelet with little marcasites in it and a tiny ruby. I got it from my special second-hand shop down near Wood Green, which sells gorgeous things at an actual reasonable price. I keep it to myself, as I don't want the shop swamped with busybody folk who'll drive the prices up.

I reach Minnie's at noon and see that there are two flutes of fizz already on the table, along with two bowls of sweet potato fries. Fuck me, another non-diet day. I'm going to look like a ten-ton wagon soon. Elsa has a twinkle in her eye that I don't think I've seen in years. Some of it must be relief. But something else too . . . hope?

'Hey, handsome, you look very sparkly,' I say to her. 'What's going on? And thanks for the pre-order. Yum.'

I snaffle a chip and join Elsa as she raises her glass.

'A new adventure! By the way, I bought these boots in celebration of soon having more money to play with . . . *Salute*.'

I take a sip, then waggle my finger at her.

'Aren't you supposed to buy things *after* you've reduced your debt?'

'Tanz, you really do let yourself get caught up in minor details.'

There's nothing I can do but laugh and take another sip. Elsa looks so much perkier. Her skin is glowing and she's lost the tightness at the sides of her mouth.

'You look excited to be going. It'll be so weird not having you in the area.'

'I'm bricking it, to be honest, but I know I have a good job waiting there for me for as long as I want, provided I don't blow it. I have a couple of mates waiting to take me for a drink and, best of all, the dog rescue centre there is full of gorgeous pooches that need a home. I don't know how I'm going to narrow it down to just one, but the second day I get there I'm booked to go in and meet them all.'

She takes another mouthful of champagne and grins happily.

'I've wasted so much time on unkind men. Suddenly all I can think about is having a nice safe place to live and a dog or two to love. I don't think I even care about men any more. I'm certainly not sparing them too much thought. Usually, I'd be wondering what hotties might be available in the new location. Not this time. I'm only glad it's a new build, so no ghosts.'

I daren't tell her that ghosts can come with the ground that the flat is built on, rather than the building itself. Instead, I raise my glass.

'Here's to your new life and me never seeing you again, because I'm allergic to dogs.'

'*What?*'

'Jesus, can a girl not joke any more?'

It wasn't a joke about my allergy to dogs, but an antihistamine is all it takes to calm the wheeze and the rash for twelve hours. If I'm going to get a free stay with Elsa in Scotland, I'm not going to let a serious allergy get in the way.

'Oh, you cow. I worry about you sometimes, you know. Always hiding behind a joke, but I think you're as lonely as I am.'

I swear she has never said anything like that in all the

194

years I've known her. I down nearly half my drink in response.

'Fuck me, Elsa, when did you get into philosophy?'

'Now. I got into it now. Since I realized I've been even more depressed for years than I thought I was. Since my therapist pushed me hard and I realized how many men and colleagues, and sometimes complete strangers, I've actively encouraged to treat me badly. I didn't know of course, I didn't know I was doing it, but I was. Plus, I've realized the happy pills don't work like they did, and I don't want to up my dose. I want to down my bloody dose. And you spend at least as much time as I do on your own. I know you're not as socially fucked up as I am, but apart from Sheila, the one person you really love spending time with is Milo. And he's 284 miles away by car. I know that, because you told me one night when you were sad and pissed. Do you like it here still?'

'I . . . I love north London. I don't love . . . aspects of my life now. I feel empty.'

'I knew it! I'm sorry. I know I'm a narcissist, but I'm a nice one and I do care and I do listen. Even if I don't respond because I'm checking my eyeliner status.'

'You're not a narcissist, you're just shallow as fuck.'

'Said the actress.'

'Yes, all right. It may interest you to know that I don't love the world of acting as much as I did. But I'm not sure what I can do instead. I'm trying to work it out.'

'Oh, wow, we need another drink, pronto.' She waves at the waiter.

'That's another thing: "having another drink" seems to

be one of my main hobbies right now. I think I need to drink less,' I tell her.

'Why the fuck would anyone do that?'

'Well, for one, it's a depressant . . .'

'Exercise helps balance that.'

'And two, it makes you fat.'

'Again, exercise. But I hate that one even more. Drink *a lot* of water.'

'I do drink a lot of water, you doofus. But I think my liver should have a rest. And more importantly, what am I going to do without you? You're my last link to the bit of me that believes I'm living the cosmopolitan life in London with the "in-crowd". When I'm actually a woman in her thirties living with her cat, feeling more and more mortified as an actress because I hate making a tit of myself.'

'I knew there was something going on. You've not sounded excited about any of your acting jobs in ages, but you've sounded absolutely overjoyed to go and hang out with ghosts. You do things that would turn my hair white. That night you cleared my flat with Sheila, I was terrified. You two acted like you were out on a jaunt to the local social club. You were all, "Oh, an old lady died here in your bedroom, but she's gone now." I saw a *you* I've never seen before. And you could do it in your pyjamas and it wouldn't matter, you'd still be fierce; no need to get dressed up or do anything for show. You were naturally fabulous. I felt like a twatty, boring coward by comparison. I think it's what first got me thinking.'

'I've not thought about it like that before. No dressing up, needing to be noticed, caring how many doughnuts I've had. When I do the spooky stuff, it feels like I'm really achieving something and maybe helping in the world. Then I look at it from the outside, afterwards, and think, well, yes, it's pretty special, but nobody except those in the know would even believe it. It's a secret talent, and it will never pay my bills.'

'It could pay your bills. Think bigger, Tanz. Think of using your talents for good and having a business from them too. Still help people, but maybe write about it, or charge proper fees for ghost-busting, or work for a secret agency or something. Mix your talent with a way to pay the rent. Total charlatans seem to make millions lying about ghosts. You're the real deal, so you at least deserve to fund your wine habit while you're doing it.'

'Bloody hell, Elsa, when did you become wise?'

'You can be unutterably shallow and a hopeless spend-thrift and still be emotionally intelligent at the same time, you know.'

'No, you can't.'

'Well, I'm the exception that proves the rule. I've had some proper help and, after years of failed and pathetically expensive therapy, now I *get* it. A bit. And I think we all change and develop as we get older. My last squeeze – that guy who wouldn't shut up about auras – he said we have developmental "spans" where we change every seven years. By the time we hit forty-nine, the seven-sevens, if we haven't learned the lessons we should have learned, they start coming back thick and fast and smacking us over the head.

'We're both over thirty-five, Tanz. What if we need to

197

learn big shit before we're forty-two? I don't even want to imagine being forty-two. I never used to think I'd live past thirty. I'd at least like to think I'd found a life I could build on by then and that I'd learned some of my lessons. And *you* – you could be a spiritual diva, a word-of-mouth super-witch. Still acting, if you want, or teaching, or giving workshops on tuning into your spooky side. Not that I'd attend, as you scared the absolute shit out of me last time. I still don't want to connect with ghosts; you can do that for me.'

Bloody hell, she's making sense. It must be the drink. I reach over and grab her hand.

'I can't believe you came up with all of that on your own. I thought thinking too deeply exhausted you?'

'Cheeky cow.'

'That is a direct quote from you. I love you for it. And I've loved spending my disgraceful youth with you, lass. I don't like that you're going away and everything is changing. But I'm so glad for you.'

'You're next, Tanz.'

It's all got a bit serious and Elsa, of all people, has put me in a place where I need to reassess everything. Not knowing what else to do, I get out her gift.

'Here . . .'

'Oh my *God*, a prezzie!' She rips the paper off like an overexcited five-year-old, then squawks with excitement when she sees the bracelet.

'Oh, look at the stones.'

'That's a little ruby.'

'It's antique, I know it is – it's gorgeous. This looks so

expensive, Tanz. My favourite kind of gift. You know how I hate tat. So many people hand over cheap stuff. Why buy crappy rubbish for your friends? But this! I really love it.'

See. I knew she was in there somewhere.

THE CLÍODHNA

It's only 8 p.m. and I'm home! I switched to water after a few drinks, had a coffee, then one more fizz. Elsa was a fucking mess, but a happy one, and I ordered an Uber, took her home down the road, then got dropped back here. I know that's quite an indulgence, but this was a big thing. Elsa has always lived 'down the road', so not having her here any more will be strange.

Drinks-wise, I'm fine. We were together for ages, so the alcohol effects seem to have worn off. I make myself a lemon and ginger tea and settle on the sofa to watch a movie called *What We Do in the Shadows* again, because twenty-seven times simply isn't enough, is it? That's of course when my phone rings. I decide not to answer it, then change my mind and look at the screen. It's Neil. It stops ringing before I can answer, and soon afterwards it pings with a voicemail. I put the phone to my ear and can hear the noise of a crowded room with people talking and laughing. Then I hear Neil.

'Tanz, one of my colleagues is having goodbye drinks.

It's too loud. I wish I was watching a film full of murderers with my favourite death-pervert. I . . . erm, wanted to tell you that I really like you. You're amazing. I REALLY LIKE YOU—'

And just like that, it cuts off.

I grin and try to stifle the little flutter in my heart, then stop dead. My living-room door is half open and the passage light is off. There is a woman standing out there in the shadows cast by the candles I've lit in my living room. Inka is in the kitchen, eating her dinner, and I'm alone on my sofa with a zombie-looking woman staring straight at me in my own house. Her hair seems to be fair; her face is blackened, and her tongue protrudes. She is shrouded in a dirty sheet and is making horrible noises. She is semi-transparent, so I can't make everything out properly, but I nearly shit seven sputniks when I first spot her, and now my panic is real. This is Hammer Horror shit, and my 'fluttering with being fancied' heart just shifted to 'trying to get out of my actual chest' mode. Not knowing what else to do, I shout, 'Go away. GO AWAY.'

To my immense relief, I blink my eyes shut and open them again and she has indeed gone away. But that was a fucking staring almost-corpse. What the hell? I'm not equipped for this kind of terrifying shit. I don't even call for Frank, I simply burst into tears. When I collect myself enough, I call Sheila and honk down the phone that I'm terrified.

Ten minutes later she arrives in a cab and fills my living room, now lit by every lamp and bulb at once, with the comforting scents of fruity steam and Samsara. As I make her a tea, Sheila carefully walks around my not-very-big flat, chatting away to Inka, who follows her like a faithful lapdog. Inka adores Sheila, and vice versa.

Once we're on the sofa together, the hallway now brightly lit, she nods and sucks on her vape.

'I've felt around, love, and there's no one here. No one "haunting" the flat. Not even that nurse. I reckon you've scared her off. I think you've seen another one of the visions that are coming from Southwark. This Nelly, she is so connected with you that whoever she thinks about and tries to grab onto in her mind is being woken up. Not the person or the ghost, but the memory they left behind; you are seeing who she's looking for and, I presume, trying to talk to. The only way to stop this now is to speak to Nelly and find out what she wants.'

'It was a fucking corpse-woman staring at me, Sheils. They don't usually come as groaning corpses. Why was she black in the face, with her tongue out?'

'Strangled?'

'Oh, great, so it's now a murder thing. I promised my little mam it wasn't. She'll be on the phone again soon, having a go – you can't hide anything from her.'

I look at my mobile, fearful my mam will call any second.

'Right, Tanz, get the candles lit and the lights back out. We'll find some stuff out, then tomorrow you can go and solve this once and for all. I'll help, if you need me. I think you've had enough and, by the looks of Cross Bones Graveyard, all the walls will be rubble soon if this doesn't come to some kind of conclusion.'

'I think you're right, but do we really need to turn all the lights back out?'

'Adds a bit of atmosphere, don't you think, if it's only candles?'

'Fucksake, what if a whole legion of black-faced, swollen-tongued zombie people show up here and I can't get rid of them? The council tax'll go through the roof, for a start.'

We both laugh, but I'm genuinely nervous. Sheila stays on the sofa and I sit in my armchair, after bringing it closer and putting a little side table with two candles on it between us. I'm extremely loath to switch off the hall light, so I leave it on, but close the living-room door. We sit quietly for a few seconds until Sheila speaks up calmly.

'I now pull up a protection around Tanz and myself. Only the positive and the helpful can speak to us and offer assistance. Those who mean ill or want mischief are not only not welcome near us, they are not welcome in this flat and will not be admitted henceforth. Now, please. Tanz needs assistance in working out what exactly is required of her. We've been told she needs to find someone called Nelly and speak to her, is that correct?'

'*Correct.*'

We both hear it. A London twang with a hint of Irish. Like the woman I could hear on the sewing machine. The one in the dark, in my dream, who asked, '*Is it really you?*' We can hear her in the room, rather than inside our heads. This is new to me, but compared with the scary woman in my hallway, I can handle it. Especially with Sheila here. I decide to let Sheila do most of the talking.

'Hello, can you tell me who you are?'

'I'm Bronagh, daughter of Brid.'

I gasp. 'Sheila, Brid is the little girl, Oonah's niece, the one who knocked on the door across the road from the graveyard and got food from Kath, the knitter! The only ones who lived, in that family I saw, remember?'

'Hello, Bronagh. Tanz and I are grateful you're here. Can you tell us something of what's going on?'

'I don't know everything. But she's confused . . . my daughter, Nelly.'

Now it makes sense. The sewing-machine lady, Bronagh, was Nelly's mum. Brid was Nelly's grandma.

'Brid, my ma, had a hard life. Oonah went to the workhouse. After she saw her brother dug back up in the graveyard, she was no good to anybody. She never got over her family dying and she couldn't concentrate on anything, she was so distressed.'

'Oh, Brid – I think I saw her, but didn't realize, in the workhouse, ill on the floor with lots of other people. I saw it in a dream. She died then?'

'She did. But old Kath took in my ma and saw her right 'til she was sixteen, but then old Kath herself died and her son was a bit too free with his hands, if you see what I mean, so Brid – my ma – had to make her own way. She had learned the art of sewing from Kath, before her eyes gave out, so she was lucky to get a job as a seamstress. Not much money at first, but she got really good and married well in the end, to a butcher's son. She hated all the blood, but suddenly she had a respectable life. Her husband took over the shop when his dad retired, and Ma made babies. Like a

curse, six of 'em died. I was second-last, when my ma was in her late thirties. I was the first one that lived. She had one more, my brother, George; she was forty-five then and he was the one that finished her off.'

'Oh, I'm so sorry, Bronagh.'

'Don't you be worrying. I was in a better place than my other family had been, and my ma told me all the stories. Plus, she had married well enough that I made a respectable marriage to a tailor with his own shop. Eventually I had a sewing machine and had three strong babies. I was thirty-three when Nelly came. Prettiest little thing you ever saw. My husband was a forward-thinking man, I'm proud to say, so we stopped having children after three because it weakened me, and we made every effort to keep them well and strong. Nelly was the youngest and she's outlived the other two by a good forty years.'

'Thank you so much, Bronagh. Tanz has been seeing a lot of activity and we've both witnessed plenty of things happening in Cross Bones. Do you know why?'

'It's the family history, isn't it? Passed from Oonah, through my ma, down to me and then to Nelly. Oonah didn't want the death of her family to mean nothing, so she passed the stories on to us. She missed Ireland something terrible . . .'

I think back to being on the floor in that horrible room, listening to the illness around, shitting and vomiting, and mostly I remember the yearning. Oonah's yearning for the countryside. Wishing to be home again in happier times. How sad for her. How I wish I could have helped.

'My beautiful daughter is old now. Old and dying. She

helped broken children and raised money for them as long as she could. But now most of the people she knew are dead, and her mind's wandering the back streets of the old stories she was told. She's always lived in Southwark and she's going to die there. I think she's exploring the stories she held close, looking to speak to the past. But she's made of magic, my girl, more than she knows, and it's causing all kinds of trouble. More than anything, she wants to speak to the Clíodhna again.'

Sheila glances at me, mystified.

'The what, Bronagh?'

'*Clíodhna. The sacred one who spoke to our family through the ages. It was the Clíodhna who told Oonah to get water from another place. No one listened, but my ma was tiny and asleep, and Oonah walked and got new water, so by the time Brid was awake, they drank that instead. It was too late for the rest of them – they drank from the first lot. When they got sick, Oonah did what she could and remembered to wash her hands. Told my ma too. Saved them, Oonah said. Said the Clíodhna fed them too, after the funeral. Ma said the Clíodhna sent them to a stranger's door, and that stranger was old Kath.*'

Sheila looks meaningfully at me. I'm completely shocked. They thought it was some kind of supernatural being or magical thing and it was only plain old me, spouting whatever shit came into my mind. Wow! 'The Clíodhna' – I feel very honoured.

'*I was gone by the time my Nelly's Robert got killed in the war. My heart gave out the day after my fifty-eighth birthday. My Ted had already gone; he was much older, and consumption had taken him. Nelly was left with her husband and her brother, who was also at war and didn't come back. The day her house was bombed was the day she was in despair. She'd just lost Robert and she didn't have me to comfort her. That day she heard the Clíodhna, who spoke with Nelly and gave her comfort, then gave her the greatest gift of all: words with her husband. She has been forever grateful. I think she might be looking for the Clíodhna. Looking to be taken to Robert. The Clíodhna promised she'd be reunited with Robert.'*

Holy fuck, this is crazy. She's wandering around the back streets of her mind and history, looking for me! And if she is who I think she is, she's already met me. Sheila looks very curious suddenly.

'Bronagh, did you ever speak to the Clíodhna?'

'No. But once I was working at my machine and I could hear breathing. Calm and kind breathing. I asked if she was there and she didn't reply. But that night I left out whisky and fruit as an offering to her. Just so she knew I appreciated her.'

This is giving me goosebumps. That, again, was me. If I try to think about time and space like this, and get all *Donnie Darko* about it, I may well faint with the brainache. Instead, I move us swiftly on.

'Bronagh, hello, I'm Tanz. I really want to help Nelly. Do you know, was she the one I met outside Cross Bones Graveyard a few weeks ago?'

'She wears a blue hat, my girl. With a matching coat. Like a pretty little doll.'

'Oh my god, Sheila, it's her. We did meet. I need to find

her. I know which block she lives in. I might simply knock on all the doors.'

Another question suddenly occurs to me.

'Bronagh. Tanz again, is there someone in your family history who was strangled to death?'

'*Not that I am aware of. They died in other gruesome ways instead. Murdered by the rich.*'

'Amen, sister.'

Sheila looks at me and we nod.

'Thank you so much, Bronagh, you've helped a lot. Tomorrow we shall seek your daughter and see what we can do. I'm sure Tanz can soothe her.'

'*Thank you. She's dying and her mind is disconnecting from her reason. Please comfort my girl. She's coming home soon.*'

I put my hands together and touch them to my forehead.

'Bronagh, you have an amazing family history and you are an incredible woman. Thank you for your time.'

'Yes, Bronagh, thank you for coming and talking to us. We are honoured and we will help your daughter.'

We hear her voice fading. '*Comfort her . . .*' Then she's gone.

We put the lamps back on and I get us both a glass of wine. It's surprising how tired you can feel after such a session.

'Bloody hell, Tanz. You went into family folklore. Three generations!'

'That is the most insane thing I've ever heard, and I've experienced a lot of crazy shit recently. But I have to say, I was guided; it didn't start from me. I was taken to those people and "told" what to say.'

'Whatever happened, you now know the answers, and it's time to make things right.'

'You still coming?'

'Try and stop me.'

I sip from my glass and try to shake off my last niggle.

'What about the dead ghost-woman tonight? Do you think there's someone in the family history who Bronagh doesn't know about? A missing jigsaw piece?'

'It's possible, love, or it might be someone buried in the graveyard that she accidentally activated. There are so many of them. Hopefully, all will be revealed tomorrow.'

'Hopefully.'

Unfortunately, that doesn't solve the riddle of how the fuck I'm going to get a wink of sleep tonight. Every light in this place is staying on, I know that much.

MORNING MISSION

I'm up at 6 a.m. All the lights in the flat were beaming last night of course, I'd have lit flaming torches as well if I could, but like a miracle, I slept. I think it was Sheila and me talking to Bronagh that wiped me out. Plus, I asked my guides, before I went to sleep, to give me a night off from visions and dreams. For once I was listened to, which is a miracle in itself. Frank hasn't made himself felt in the past twelve hours and I feel partly abandoned and partly like he's decided that I should start working things out without his help. Soft-voiced lass has also been noticeable by her absence. I'd have thought she would have stuck her beak straight in when Bronagh appeared last night, but who knows? Maybe all my spooky voices were having a day off yesterday.

I'm showered and ready by 6.45. I have the strongest of feelings that this mission is one that I must attend to on my own. There's no way Sheila will be up before nine anyway, if she's not working, and I'm raring to go. I'm pretty sure I should leave the house immediately, so I get my coat on and check my bag for all the essentials – flask of coffee, keys, purse, phone and a cheeky protein bar as I'm trying to repair the damage wrought by desserts, alcohol and English breakfasts. It's all there, so off I trot. The bus ride is quite pleasant. It's not rammed, there are no school kids yet and the sky is bright. I sit on the top deck at the front, like I'm driving, and when I pass the road leading to Elsa's, I feel such a pang. A pang for the past: for who I was, where I am now and what on earth will be coming next. I shake it off as the bus powers me down to the Tube; the traffic is nowhere near as horrifying as it'll be in an hour. I like this early start. Not that I could do it every day. Far too lazy.

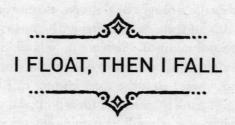

I FLOAT, THEN I FALL

London Bridge is hectic just before 8 a.m., when I exit onto Borough High Street. It's lucky I brought my own coffee as there's a queue out of the door at Costa, and all of the little cafes seem to be full of people grabbing an on-the-go breakfast. As I approach my turning onto Union Street I'm surprised to see that blanket-man is already there, looking wide awake, sitting on cardboard, blanket on his head, smiling at passers-by. When I glance in my purse, there's only a fiver there. I'm not minted enough to be handing him notes, but as I approach he speaks to me.

'Hiya, you.'

His friendly northern vowels stop me in my tracks.

'Hello, erm . . .'

'I'm Stuart.'

'Hiya, Stuart. I'm Tanz.'

'Interesting name, Tanz.'

'Thanks.'

'I've seen you a lot around here the past few weeks, Tanz. Do you work here now?'

'Ha, no, not really. I've had some business at the grave-yard. I've seen you plenty too. You live nearby?'

When he smiles, his teeth are a brownish yellow.

'Yes, lived round here fifteen years. I know everybody.'

I stop in my tracks. *Of course.*

'Really? That's interesting. There's someone I'm looking to talk to – she lives just down there, in the block with the balconies. Old lady called Nelly. You know which door is hers?'

He winks. 'I might do.'

I take the rumpled fiver out of my purse.

'I only have this, but it might get you a hot drink or something.'

'Lovely that. Thank you. Nelly lives in the orange door, number seven. She's not been around so much. Older than Ben Nevis, that one. Mind's started wandering. Like talking to an empty colander.'

He's very poetic, is this Stuart. You can see from the sparkly eyes and strong jaw that he used to be an attractive lad. I wonder what brought him to sitting on street corners, getting pissed on cheap cider and wearing a blanket on his head? I sometimes think every single one of us is but two or three steps from the same fate. I certainly am.

'Thank you, Stuart. Very helpful.'

'Any time; any other questions, you come to me. I know everything about this place.'

As I'm walking towards the orange door, it occurs to me that I should ask Stuart about Jill, the missing red-haired sister, if he's been around here for fifteen years. But then that thought is knocked out of me when I feel the whoosh of an electric volt through my body and I hear the voice of Robert, the soldier, in my head.

'*Cross Bones. Now! Cross Bones.*'

I walk fast, then break into a run. As I approach the graveyard, I see a crumpled figure on the ground. She's lying on her side and, as I get closer, I see she's quietly mouthing something to herself. There's no one walking on this side of the road, but there are plenty of cars passing, obviously suspecting she's drunk or mad, because they're not stopping. This woman in the blue coat and blue hat with the flower in it, this tiny human, is over one hundred years old – why would they leave her just lying in the street? I can almost hear the outrage of her mistreated, starved and penniless past family shouting in fury that their bloodline is still being abused. As I reach her, I see that she's ripped her tights. She's muttering, and the graveyard is vibrating with ghosts. I sit on the ground, which is cool and dusty but not littered, and lay her head in my lap. Nelly isn't bleeding, as far as I can see; she's simply fallen to the ground. She's as light as a meringue and the wisps of hair emerging from the pinned-on bucket hat are pure white. I stroke her translucent cheek. She has no colour at all. She's like a fine white porcelain doll. Her tiny, bony hand lifts and covers mine. When she speaks, her voice is so quiet that I have to bend right forward to hear it.

'Thank you. I got lost.'

The graveyard is vibrating with life. I can't see them, but I hear them. The layers upon layers of outcast dead, the moments most cherished or most traumatizing for all these beautiful souls, who were as good as anyone else, but were never allowed to believe so.

'Are you all right, Nelly?'

'I am. I just want to lie here. Do you hear them?'

'Of course I hear them. So many people who were buried here, Nelly, so many who deserved better than they got. Do you want me to get you home? You can tell me about them?'

As I speak, I see some rubble falling from the already-damaged drystone wall inside. This psychic activity in the grounds really is dislodging bricks and stones. Also, I begin to see faces – really see them, not simply in my mind's eye. They're coming to the railings of the graveyard and staring at Nelly: the dead who are ignited by her and want to get closer to her. They're mostly women, but I see her grandma's uncle, only thirteen years old at the time, who stole bread and oranges, but also brought in the bucket of death. Unlike the children who are running about happily, he looks mournful and lost. I wonder how many of Nelly's family rest in peace, after what they went through before their deaths. I begin to work out why Nelly has been looking for them. With very little effort, I pull her up to a sitting position and let her lean against me. She hooks her arm in mine.

'So tired. I float, then I fall. Why was I on the ground?'

I put my arm round her and hug her carefully, kissing her on the forehead beneath the soft brim of her hat.

'You fell over, Nelly. You need a cup of tea and a biscuit.'

A little chortle surprises me. She sounds like a cheeky toddler.

'I have some custard creams. But I like coffee.'

I pull out my flask and open the top.

'Today is your lucky day then, Nelly. It's not boiling, just nice and hot. Good homemade coffee!'

She takes the flask from me and has a few sips. Her tiny voice is suddenly more animated.

'This is good stuff. Italian?'

'Indeed.'

She looks straight up at me, and her pale eyes are sharp for a moment.

'Do I know you?'

'I don't think so.'

'You're on TV, aren't you?'

I can't help it – it's the last thing I expect, and I break into chortles. When Nelly feels my body shaking with mirth, she catches the bug and her toddler-laugh rings out. I need to help this one home. Get some sugar in her veins.

I carefully stand and reach down for her hand.

'Come on, Nelly, we need to talk.'

MIRROR BETWEEN TWO WORLDS

We walk back to Nelly's flat. Behind us the cemetery sounds like London Bridge at its busiest. I daren't look. I have my arm around Nelly's shoulder and she's leaning into me as she walks.

'They're all out this morning.'

'Yes, Nelly, they certainly are.'

'They like to be out in the sun, you see? We all like some light in the darkness.'

'You're right, we do, but I don't know if this lot need to see the light again; they've been gone a long time.'

We reach her front door and she fumbles around in her pocket for her key. When she opens up, I'm confounded by the clutter. As soon as the door opens, I can see there are newspapers and books everywhere. They're crowding the hallway on each side and are topped with ageing carrier bags filled with 'stuff'. All this forms a corridor that you have to walk down very carefully.

Nelly leads the way. The air is filled with dust, old paper and violets, with a dash of stinky kitchen. She takes me into a living room, which is piled up with magazines, news-papers and bags, with knick-knacks covering every open surface and only one seat clear enough to sit on. The seat is a moth-eaten antique chair in teal and has worn patches on the arms. It's facing an ancient TV, which stands proudly by a large old-fashioned wireless. There's also a tiny table with two wooden chairs at the window. The curtains are drawn, and I wonder if Nelly would mind if I opened them. The chairs are piled with stuff – I'll clear one if I need to sit down. I make sure Nelly is comfortable in her armchair.

'Should I make you a cuppa, Nelly?'

'Yes, please. Cafetière of coffee, and maybe a biscuit?'

'Of course! You sit there and get your strength back.'

She smiles, then her face goes completely blank.

'Who are you again?'

'I'm Tanz. I love your hat.'

'Thank you. I like blue. But it's indoors now, isn't it? Perhaps I shouldn't wear it indoors.'

'That's up to you – it's your flat.'

She smiles so sweetly at me again as I leave the room to look for the kitchen. The mess carries on everywhere. I accidentally walk into the bathroom and find it filthy, with scum in the bath and towels all over the floor. And magazines in piles here too. Historical ones, gardening ones – which is strange, considering she has no garden – photography, crime, biology . . . so many different subjects. I'm impressed. But I don't want to look at the state of the toilet bowl, so I back out, and this time I enter the kitchen.

There are several bin bags that haven't been taken out. The sink is filled with bowls. Just bowls. There's one cup.

It's not washed, but I'm guessing it's Nelly's favourite. When I look in the fridge I find a pile of micro-meals. Mostly spaghetti Bolognese. But there is also a bag of coffee, a cafetière that needs rinsing out and a biscuit barrel. A proper one, like my mam has. I look inside and nearly laugh. Custard creams, Jammie Dodgers and Gypsy creams. I get a plate. I cannot wait to snaffle down a couple of Gypsy creams – I love them. This kitchen is the smelliest room, from all the old food in black bin bags. I suspect Nelly's sense of smell isn't great, but whose is, at over one hundred years old? She's an absolute miracle at this age, wandering around the streets, forming full sentences with her tiny gentle voice. And her eyes . . . I love her pale eyes.

I find a tin tray and put on it the cafetière, her cup (I've rinsed it), another one that I find in the cupboard and a plate of biscuits. I'm at the door of the living room when I look at Nelly, sitting in the curtained gloom, and try not to drop the tray when I see a woman standing five feet away from her. I know who it is as soon as I see her. It's Oonah. But Oonah isn't speaking to Nelly; she's standing, scream- ing at someone we can't see.

'*My boy, my lovely boy . . . You pulled him back out. Why? His head – look at what you did.*'

Nelly is watching the action like it's a film. She looks entranced and mortified at the same time. She's crying. I walk to the little Formica side table next to her and put down the tray.

'Coffee!'

Oonah disappears and Nelly turns to me, tears still on her cheeks.

'Did you bring biscuits?'

'Of course. What's your favourite?'

'The jam ones.'

I should be elated that I'll get all the Gypsy creams to myself, but the sight of Oonah screaming in a graveyard more than a hundred and fifty years ago has very much screwed up my head. I pour us both a coffee.

'Milk, Nelly?'

'A little.'

'Do you see Oonah a lot, Nelly?'

She sips her coffee and I clear a wooden chair, piling magazines onto the table, then place it next to the tray and Nelly, and sit down.

'My family. The things they went through.'

'I know. It wasn't nice.'

'I see them. In the mirror.'

'Which mirror?'

'This – my mirror. The rooms.'

I think she means her flat. In the curtained gloom, cup in hand, another of my dream visits becomes reality. We're now in another room together, Nelly and me. The man in the bed, the baby in the crib with the rag over it. But instead of me being the woman in the scenario, I can see her. Fair hair, slender frame, sad eyes, wiping her husband's forehead.

'Oonah's other sister, her big sister. Lost her husband, then her baby died.'

'Oh, Nelly, it's so sad. What happened to her?'

Nelly turns to me, her eyes moist. This situation is incredible – we're in the room. It smells of bodily functions, it's cold and there's noise outside. The people aren't quite solid, but damn close, and it's like we shot back in time and landed here. I feel like Doctor bloody Who.

'She became ill after she lost them both. Drowned herself.'

'Oh no!'

This makes sense regarding the state of grief Oonah's family seemed to be in when they were huddled together in that room. They'd lost Oonah's sister – who must already have lived in Southwark – to suicide, as well as fleeing the famine. How much sadness could one family take? A lot more, if my visions were anything to go by.

'I think about her a lot and she just comes. Is she all right? I ask if she's all right, but she doesn't answer. Why won't she talk to me?'

As Nelly speaks in her wispy, kindly voice, the room changes again. It's incredible – the graveyard. I find it hard to look down. The semi-rotted corpse on the ground, head detached. Old man standing guiltily as Oonah, her face contorted, screams and screams in the drizzle. The smell is different from that in the room we just left: rotted flesh, industrial smoke and soot and something else. Something that must be coming from the river.

Nelly takes a biscuit, like she sees this all the time.

'I go to the graveyard and try to tell her I love her: Oonah. I try to help her. But she doesn't hear. She didn't get over this. Went quite mad. She was in the workhouse. Died there. Luckily my grandmother had somewhere to go. They put Oonah in Cross Bones too. She didn't want to be buried in that awful place where they'd dig you back up.'

The vision fades, the smell lingering longer than the picture.

'Yes, Nelly. Brid went to old Kath's.'

Nelly looks at me in wonder.

'You know old Kath?'

'I know a lot of things.'

She suddenly reaches out and takes my hand. The rush of emotion I feel as she does so gives me some indication of how much Nelly's been carrying on her own. I also feel huge confusion. At her age, it's only natural that her mind is wandering. She's lucky still to be mobile and even semi-lucid. There's something else I can 'feel' as I hold her hand. She's between two worlds, which is why she can see what she can, and why I can see it with her. Nelly is halfway to their world. It's incredible. And it's magnifying my connection too. She smiles at me.

'I had a friend . . .'

Suddenly I see a red-haired lass I recognize. She's dunking a biscuit into her coffee and is sitting at the table in this very room, seemingly listening and laughing at a story she's being told.

'Nelly, is that Jill?'

As quickly as I see it, it's gone, and Nelly stares at me in confusion.

'She's fading.'

'Oh, hello soft-voiced lass. What do you mean by "fading"?'

'Nelly should have died a long time ago. She has pushed through and stayed here through sheer will alone. She has

many underlying ailments, and most people would have died of full organ failure by now.'

'So why is she still here?'

'Fear. Nelly's not seen or heard from her husband Robert since that one time in the war. Not fully. She's felt his presence, but not "heard" him. Plus, she's confused. All the stories in her head that were fed through the generations – she used to tell those stories to anyone who would listen. But then her good friend died ten years ago and it damaged her; she was lost. She internalized it all. She connects with the past in the way only an old Irish witch can, but she doesn't realize her power. She's lonely. The past has become her friend, so she plays and replays it, but only sad things; and she doesn't realize what she's awakening when she's between two planes like this.'

'How do you know all this?'

'I just do.'

'What can I do?'

'Talk to her, Tanz. You can bridge all those gaps for her. Then she can leave.'

I smile at Nelly, who's on her second biscuit, and take a bite of a Gypsy cream.

'Nelly, what are you looking for?'

'What do you mean?'

'All of these sad memories from your family's past.'

'Yes. They weren't treated right. They're lost and upset. I want to know how they are. I lost my mammy . . .'

Suddenly she sings a sweet, whispery lament. One that echoes from the past:

'I've found my bonny babe a nest On Slumber Tree,
I'll rock you there to rosy rest, Asthore Machree
Oh, lulla lo, sing all the leaves On Slumber Tree,
'Til everything that hurts or grieves Afar must flee.
I've put my pretty child to float Away from me,
Within the new moon's silver boat On Slumber Sea.
And when your starry sail is o'er From Slumber Sea,
My precious one, you'll step to shore On Mother's
    knee.'

'That was lovely, Nelly. Where did you learn that?'

'My mother used to sing it. She could sing . . . Where is my mother? Where did she go? Mother?'

I heard her mother sing that very song, of course, as I woke from a dream in a darkened room and heard her at her sewing machine.

'Your mother used to make dresses, didn't she, Nelly?'

Suddenly in front of us is a woman at a sewing machine. The rest of the room is invisible, but there sits a handsome woman with a broad figure and nimble fingers, hair pinned back in curls, seemingly making a long skirt.

Nelly reaches out her hand to the almost-solid woman and whimpers like a child.

'There she is! My mother. Look how lovely she was. I miss her. I miss her . . . They all die. Everyone dies. All the seconds you have together. Kiss the seconds.'

Her eyes seem to change now. The lucidity fades and, as it does, the room fills. It starts with children. I can see them, playing in the filth on the narrow streets. Then it's the poor beggars, sitting in doorways, caps and mugs in hand, scabs on faces, cheeks hollowed out. It makes me think of Stuart with the blanket on his head, who has begged here for years. Always the same in the world. People with much, and people with little . . . But Stuart, thank goodness, isn't suffering from some awful, now-easily-preventable physical disease, as far as I can tell. I decide I'll give him a twenty the next time I see him. Buy him a load of cider – it's the very least I can do.

As more and more people fill the room, I become aware of women who must have lived hundreds of years ago, in beds and on chaises with 'gentlemen'. Gentlemen with their breeches down round their knees and ankles, reeking of booze. I hear bears and cockerels, and screams of drunken laughter. Babies keening, and men and women crying in despair. The noise, like the graveyard that night, becomes unbearable – the people, layer upon layer of early death and fast-lived lives. I can't help wondering, as I put my hands over my ears, what the hell all these people got out of life when everything was so hard? I have to shout to be heard over the din.

'Nelly! I want to help you see Robert!'

On hearing this, she focuses again. The noise and people disappear with a snap.

'You know my husband?'

'Yes, I do. But to talk to him, we must clear up everything else. Do you think you could make it to the graveyard again, if I helped you?'

'Of course – I pass it every day. Just let me visit the water closet.'

I love how she uses the oldest of old-fashioned terms. As

she hobbles out of the room, I check my phone and find a text from Louisa from ten minutes ago:

The graveyard's gone mad. Chris ran out and won't come back, and another wall has cracked. It feels like small earthquakes. Lots of them. Can you help? Heather's freaking out.

Now I know what's been happening. While a confused elderly psychic with the power of two worlds at her beck has been scrolling through her ancestors' lives and beyond – all of them involved with the local cemetery – she's been linking in with everyone who died there, instead of merely those she sought, and her emotions as she watched their hard, unkind lives have literally been shaking the ground. I had no idea it was possible, but there are plenty of things in the past year of my life that I can't explain in the slightest. And this lady, like lots of other people, just needs help and love. She's been dealing with things she didn't understand all on her own. Now, hopefully, I can help. My only worry is that she'll lose lucidity. I reply to Louisa:

I'm on my way. Be there in the next few minutes and I'm bringing a special guest. Could you make a bench or chair comfortable, please, as she's very old?

A few moments later Nelly comes back in, hat and coat on, slick of shakily applied crimson lipstick on.

'You look beautiful, Nelly.'

'Why thank you, erm . . .'

'Tanz. Don't worry, it's a weird name. Call me what you like – I'll answer.'

Nelly's laugh is so cute when it comes. She's like a little windchime, turning from one mood to another on the breeze. I get up and put my arm around her.

'Come on then. Let's go visiting.'

LET THE DEAD REST

Louisa is waiting as I walk painfully slowly towards the gate with my precious cargo. I say 'cargo' because I'm pretty much carrying Nelly, but she's so light, it's no trouble. Louisa smiles when she sees Nelly and obviously knows her.

'Well, hello, Nell. How are you?'

'I'm very well indeed, I met a new friend. She has a strange name – I keep forgetting it.'

This tickles me a lot and I kiss Nelly on the forehead again. I know it might be patronizing, but she's so fucking cute. She almost purrs when she gets a kiss, so I don't think she minds. Louisa helps me lead Nelly to the bench, which she has covered with a shawl and has draped another over the back, to make it a little softer. Louisa is such a considerate person. I love it when the world reminds me of people's kindness. Heather is here too, standing next to the end wall, drinking from a Styrofoam cup and looking very displeased. She waves and nods, then makes her way over.

'Hi, Heather, this is Nelly.'

Heather smiles as best she can, despite the worry in her eyes.

'Hello again, Nelly. You've not been in for a while. Though I've seen you walking past.'

Nelly sits on her prepared seat and smiles regally around her.

'Yes, I've been rather busy, you see. Visiting my family. No time to stop. But this nice girl has brought me for a visit.'

Heather looks searchingly at me. I glance gatewards.

'Yes, Heather, Nelly's been visiting her relatives. Turns out a lot of them are buried here. It might be a good idea to maybe go get yourself another cuppa and lock the gate behind you? Unless you want to stick around.'

Heather widens her eyes in acknowledgement.

'I think I might go and sort some things in the office for an hour. Leave you to it?'

'Okay. What about you, Louisa?'

'Are you kidding? I'm staying.'

I snigger. She's like the sorcerer's apprentice. Only way sassier. We both watch as Heather leaves, each of us with a protective hand on Nelly. Seemingly she is loving the touch and the attention, as she leans into the warmth of our hands.

'It's so nice to be out with friends. But look at the nasty gravedigger over there. He upset Oonah. No wonder she looks miserable. We don't like him, do we?'

I look to the far corner in the shadows, and I see him. Louisa emits a little gasp, so she must see him too. He is slightly stooped and coughing. His face is etched with all kinds of unhappiness and his hands look filthy from here.

I put a protection over all three of us, then I ask for help and information. I don't know where it's coming from – it's not Frank or soft-voiced lass. It's an androgynous voice and quiet, but very clear.

'*His name is Simon. He's been a gravedigger for years, it's all he knows. His guilt, as he died, was enormous. Because of Oonah.*'

'Ladies, this is Simon.'

Simon is no imprint, as he looks straight up at me when I say his name. Nelly makes a disapproving noise.

'He upset Oonah. Made her ill.'

I sit by Nelly and stroke her back; she is not taking her eyes off the spectre. Louisa sits on the other side.

'Yes, Nelly, but not on purpose. He was ordered to do it by the parish. It was priests who did all of this. Just like they put the Winchester Geese to work. Simon was ordered to dig bodies back up so that more could be buried. He was poor and sick also.'

'Poor Oonah, my poor Oonah . . .'

I pat Nelly to bring her back from her reverie.

'Nelly, I think we should tell Simon that he doesn't have to stay here any more. He's not going to hell, is he? Just for doing what he was told? He died so sadly, feeling so sorry about Oonah. He thinks he's bad. He's been here all these years, feeling bad.'

Nelly looks straight at him, addresses him herself.

'Are you sad?'

Simon hangs his head, coughs again, like a dying stray dog.

'I feel the sad – the sad is so strong in this man, Tam.'

I don't correct her; 'Tam' is close enough.

'Should we let him go, Nelly?'

'I think we should. How do we do it?'

'I'll speak and you agree, okay? Convince him. He believes he deserves only hell.'

'Simon. Simon, we are sorry you had such a hard life. And we know you were told to dig up the bodies of the dead and it was part of your job. Oonah is gone now – gone to her brother – and she didn't curse you, I promise. You don't have to stay here. You can go to your maker. There is a light waiting for you.'

He opens his mouth and a strangled, chesty voice replies.

'I am damned.'

He hangs his head again and Nelly stirs and points.

'No. You have good in you – I feel it. The good aren't damned. They're not damned at all. Those who keep bad secrets are damned. That isn't you.'

'Simon, it's time to go to the next place now,' I tell him. 'Where it's light and there's no illness. You'll feel like a young man again. We all want to help, don't we?'

We all nod, and I channel as much love to him as I can. Simon feels something of it as he straightens, then looks to his left at the blank corner wall. He speaks once more, his voice registering surprise.

'What's that?'

I can't suppress a smile.

'Go and look, Simon. It's time to leave the sadness behind.'

He gawps at us, with the wonder of a little boy in his

eyes, then turns and steps through the wall. One minute there, then 'poof!' – gone.

Nelly swings her legs on the seat.

'Oh my, he went to the good place! Look. All gone!'

I glance at Louisa, whose face is shining with emotion. Her bottom lip is wobbling.

'He went.'

I smile at her. 'Yes, he did.'

I hear it in my head before I feel the heaviness of a powerful spirit approaching.

'Oonah's here.'

I look round and from a spot ten feet away, I see a light rising from the ground. I suspect this is where Oonah was buried. There's an 'Oooh' from Louisa, and Nelly's eyes are suddenly like plates.

'An angel, Tam! An angel is here.' It's all I can do to stop her scrambling down from the seat.

'Sure is. Just wait until you see who the angel is.'

Oonah takes perfect form, but she glows, and blueish light surrounds her. And she's not alone. Standing by her, with her arm over his shoulder, is her brother, also with an impressive glow, but his is more orange. He doesn't look mournful now, not at all.

'Hello, Nelly.'

'My Oonah. You look beautiful. Not upset at all.'

'Nelly, thank you for caring for us so much. Thank you for loving us. You have made all the family proud. Working with all those children who had no one else. You saved and shaped them. And not one of them died like I did. Uncared for and alone.'

Nelly looks at me, confused.

'Did I do that?'

'You must have, Nelly, or she wouldn't say it.'

'*Now I'm here with Ned, to help you. You have done everything you could to be kind. And we can't watch you be lonely any more, can we, Ned?*'

Ned gives a cheeky grin.

'*You've been the bravest of brave girls, Nelly, but now you've got to let it all go. The dead need to rest.*'

Nelly nods and I resist a rather insistent lump that's forming in my throat. I move my hand to her shoulder, and she puts her little claw on top of mine.

'Nelly, you need to let them all go now. Say whatever comes into your heart to release all those caught up in your energy.'

'My what, Tam?'

'Just say goodbye to all the people who need to rest, Nelly. It's not good waking up their memories. They've moved on. Nobody wants their last, most private feelings trapped in a graveyard, do they?'

Nelly looks up at me, then towards the smiling figures of Oonah and Ned – so different from the sad, bent-up, starving figures I've seen in my visions and dreams.

'I like to see you smile, Oonah and Ned. I thought you were in torment.'

Oonah glows brighter. I think she's feeding her light and strength to Nelly to keep her mind sharp for this task. There are semi-transparent people everywhere now, like imprints on a polaroid. The outcast dead, living out long-past moments on this Earth.

Oonah speaks gently, her face radiating warmth.

'It was not an easy life, Nelly. But you're seeing me as I am now. I left that time behind. Before, you saw the sad moments we all left behind. Tell them all they can rest now. These were private moments now passed, not for others to see.'

Nelly clears her throat. 'I'll try.'

She looks at me and I nod encouragingly.

'It's time to let go of all the ones I've woken up. I'm sorry, I haven't been right in myself and I've been doing some strange things, come to think of it. I'm letting go of all of you now. I'm sorry I woke you up. Go in peace and love. Let the dead rest.'

It's not what she says, but what happens as she says it that has Louisa and me staring at each other in shock. The ground moves. Just a tremor, a little shake, but it definitely moves. And her eyes. Her eyes glow, a pale blue like Oonah's light. And Nelly repeats her last word.

'Rest.'

As she does, all the extra bodies in the graveyard disappear. All at once. All gone. Only Oonah and Ned are left. And Nelly looks at them now, her eyes still shining.

'Did I do it? Did I do well?'

Oonah beams at her.

'You have done more than well, Nelly. Your mother will be very proud.'

'That's wonderful. But my Robert . . . I'm frightened . . . I haven't spoken to him since the Clíodhna brought him. All these years, and the Clíodhna and Robert – they didn't speak to me again. What if they've abandoned me? What if . . . what if he's not waiting? I miss him.'

'Everyone is waiting for you, Nelly. Why don't you ask the Clíodhna yourself?'

Nelly stares at this vision of Oonah, her face non-plussed. Oonah raises one arm and points to me. Louisa is now looking completely lost. Nelly looks at me hard.

'You?'

I smile and stroke her hand.

'I'm sorry not to tell you before. I saw you in the ruins of your street and I knew you were important, so I spoke to you. Told you that you would help so many others.'

'Then you brought Robert . . . How?'

'I don't know, Nelly. I have no idea what's going on half the time.'

'I . . . recognize your voice now. How can the Clíodhna also be a girl from the TV?'

I chuckle and she grins at me. I feel Robert arrive, as my left ear gets very hot.

'Robert's here, Nelly.'

Her face lights up even more.

'Robert!'

I turn to my left and suddenly he's there, five feet away – no bullet mark or blood – smiling at his wife. I hear Louisa whisper, 'The soldier.' He beckons Nelly and begins to move away. Nelly jumps from the seat and follows him. She turns and looks over her shoulder at me.

'Thank you, my Clíodhna. You saved my life that time. And now I have my Robert!'

She reaches him and he bends towards her ear. Whatever

they are saying, the delight is radiating from both of them. Standing next to Oonah and Ned is Nelly's mother, Bronagh, glowing just like them, on the concrete. Nelly hasn't noticed yet as she giggles with her husband.

I look to Louisa, who is radiating emotion. I nod at her and then catch the movement as Nelly suddenly falls to the ground. I already know she won't be getting up again. I run to her and cradle her head. Her smile is beaming, her voice fading.

'You did as you promised. I love you, my Clíodhna.'

Her eyes close for the last time. I look to Robert and there is a glowing, almost transparent version of Nelly holding his hand, now the age she was when I saw her in the ruins, and in the same dress. She looks towards Oonah, Ned and her mother, and I hear a far-off cry of happiness. Bronagh waves her thanks to me and, as Robert and Nelly reach her, the whole vision fades.

Louisa comes to the other side of Nelly, drops to the ground, takes her hand and weeps.

'Are you okay, Louisa?'

'I've never seen anything like it. Such beauty. I can't, I can't . . .'

I smile a broken mess of a smile.

'I've never seen anything like it either, mate. If we both saw it, I guess you're a medium too, whether you like it or not. Nelly has upped your powers.'

I kiss Nelly's forehead one last time. I suppose it would be nice to all die smiling like she has. Beautiful little Nelly.

IS IT DONE?

Louisa's mate Gino in the little Italian place is a bit disconcerted because she can't stop crying. I've tipped him the wink and told him it's okay, but he still looks worried. We had to wait for the ambulance for quite a while, and Louisa explained that Nelly had been a regular visitor to the graveyard and had simply collapsed. No one looked surprised as they picked up and took away the tiny shell that recently contained the mighty Nelly. Louisa gave her contact details, and all of the arrangements for her funeral and so on will be passed on soon enough.

Louisa wipes her eyes and explains something in Italian to Gino. We order coffee, then she says something else and he brings us coffees and a limoncello each. I grab her ankle under the table with both of my feet and blow a raspberry at her.

'You're going to have to get used to this psychic stuff, I reckon. You're a natural.'

'Sorry, Tanz – all of that love, it got to me. It was so

beautiful. And Nelly looked so happy. Does this mean we all get to live happily ever after, then?'

'Fuck knows! I mean, you say that, but Nelly had to wait going on eighty years to see her husband again. Doesn't seem like she had anyone else. I mean, that's a long wait for the "happy ever after".'

'I'm sure she had happy times in between in those years. We just didn't see them. We saw her at the end.'

'True.'

Louisa holds up her little shot of yellow liquid.

'To life!'

'Life!'

It has a sweet, lemony burn. Suddenly two plates of homemade lasagne are put down in front of us.

'I hope you don't mind, Tanz – thought it might ground us to have something to eat.'

'See! You're even thinking like a medium now!'

I tuck in, realizing I'm famished. What a strange turn of events. So now I can see 'them' with my eyes, instead of simply inside my head. My big question is: will I be able to see them like that all the time, or was Nelly amplifying everything with the power she didn't even realize she had?

Louisa's mind seems to be in the same place.

'Am I going to be able to see things like that from now on? I'm not sure I could do it on my own. I might have a nervous breakdown. I'm actually scared of this stuff, as well as loving it.'

'I'm currently wondering that myself. We'll see. But remember something I've learned over a whole year of craziness: sometimes we're scared of things because we've been told they're frightening, and it takes a leap of faith to realize we're not scared at all when it comes down to it. I've had to accept things I would never have believed, as if they were completely normal. Maybe you're scared because you already know this is something you can do, but it means a big change in perception and the way you live, in order to apply yourself to it.'

'Can I keep in touch with you?'

'Of course you can, you silly onion. We've just been through a war together!'

'Actually, Tanz, that's a thought. Is it done? No more walls falling in?'

I put out my 'feelers'. I am almost certain the graveyard is completely cleared. I can feel no energy coming from that direction at all.

'Yes, I think you're safe. Even the gravedigger who was probably haunting the place for years has gone. Heather and the team can start repairing the walls now. You're going to miss the drama a bit, aren't you?'

'Yes! I think I am.'

'Well, not to worry you, but once you're tuned into this nonsense, it comes to find you. This isn't your last adventure.'

Louisa's eyes fill with tears again.

'What an honour to see such incredible things.'

She's quite right. And as we finish our food, I think of Neil and last night's voicemail. Liking someone, and going for it, also takes a leap of faith and it's scary too. He hasn't bored me to tears yet, and I love how he kisses. Fuck it. I take out my phone and rattle off a text to him:

I like you too, you beautiful freak.

It has barely gone when my phone pings back:

**You've made a shit day at work a whole lot better.
When do I see you again?**

I think about this. It would be lovely to show up whatever time his shift finishes tonight and kiss his face off, but I can at least show a tiny bit of restraint. Also, I suspect I may have a few more tears saved up for what just happened. Yes, I saw Nelly go off with her husband, but realistically Louisa and I watched someone die. Nelly was in my arms when she breathed her last. I need to process that:

**I just cleared a whole graveyard of ghosts. Let me
know when you're free after tonight, and I'll let you
know.**

I go to put the phone in my pocket and it pings one more time:

**Fuck me! No one could ever be bored with you
around.**

He's got that right.

I switch my phone to silent and decide to have a quiet walk before I get the Tube.

LOOSE THREAD

I wander down to the *Golden Hinde* and sit on the same wall I sat on with Sheila last week. It's a mild enough day and it's nice to watch people milling about. It's hard to believe how much hardship people endured in Southwark for all those years, as I look around at the thriving middle-classness of it now. I love it here, where old buildings meet new, and the replica boat sits resplendent next to the pub and Southwark Cathedral.

Strangely, even though I visit here a lot, I've never been inside the cathedral and I suspect, after the morning I've had, if I walked in there now I'd see all sorts of people who died a very long time ago. Nelly has 'activated' me all right. It feels like there's a tight energy being pumped around my blood and, to be quite honest, I'd like a rest from spooks for the afternoon.

I'm still left with two questions, though. Who was that frightening zombie woman in my hallway last night, lurking in the shadows? That auntie of Brid, the one who lost her husband and baby. She had fair hair, from what I saw in

Nelly's living room. But Nelly said she drowned, and this woman had a blackened face. Maybe Nelly didn't know the full story. Maybe something worse than suicide befell the poor woman.

And why did Jill, Charlie's sister, never once register on my spook radar, but then suddenly appear, all smiles, in Nelly's memory store? I think she must have had her reasons for running off, and I think her brother may have to accept that she doesn't want to be found. I'll definitely ask blanket-man if I see him, because I intend to flash him some cash anyway, but I really do think it's a dead end, so to speak, and I don't like loose threads. I find them annoying.

Suddenly, as I'm musing, I think of Nelly's little hand in mine and get all choked up again. Being this close to death isn't fun. I just have to remember that she isn't in that hollowed-out ancient shell on a slab somewhere. She's gone.

IT'S TIME

I'm just wandering to London Bridge Tube when I get a feeling, clear as crystal, to head back to Cross Bones Graveyard. I can't believe it – I literally thought I was done. What on earth can have happened now? I'm not tired – the day's shenanigans have hyped me up, if anything – but honestly speaking, I would like to get back to north London and escape Southwark for the foreseeable future, as it's all been a bit intense. I can't ignore the clear words in my head, though: *'Go back, go back.'*

It sounds like the androgynous voice from the graveyard earlier. I really can't resist when I get this kind of explicit instruction; as Sheila said, it only causes more hassle in the end to resist, so I roll my eyes and make my way back towards Union Street.

'Why do I have to go back?'

'She's calling you.'

Jesus! Creepy much? I don't know who 'she' is, but maybe some extra aunt didn't get cleared from the graveyard and is waiting for me with a scary blackened face. I

243

walk down Union Street, past Nelly's flat, knowing that she'll never walk through that door again, wondering fleetingly who the hell will have to clear up her hoarded mess. Then I reach the end of the road and the voice surprises me by saying, *'Turn left.'*

I find myself walking in the opposite direction, away from the graveyard, up Redcross Way. Until I hear it again, clear as a bell . . .

'Here.'

I'm standing on a corner, just past the little railway bridge. It's a large building with boarded-up windows. It looks like an old pub and must have been a lovely place in its day. The windows are huge and arched and there's a stonework sign saying, 'Built in 1860', which isn't long after Cross Bonès closed for good. I look up to the second floor, which is what I'd guess consisted of accommodation over the pub; then there's another window on part of the third floor, with what I'm thinking might be a roof terrace making up the rest, though it's walled, and I can't see that far up. Must be a nice view from there. I'm not sure what I'm doing here, though. I walk from the front to the side and see an exit doorway boarded up from the inside.

'Push it.'

This is getting dodgy now. What if someone sees me and thinks I'm trying to break in? Granted, I don't look like a typical burglar, but this is still wrong. I poke my finger at the flimsy wood and it moves a bit. I push with the palm of my hand and realize that it pushes inwards and is hinged at the top. That's odd. Someone must have done that to fool people. With a good shove, I could get it open enough to sneak in.

'Why are you trying to get me to go in? Isn't this place derelict?'

'I will guide you.'

'Are you going to get me in trouble?'

'I will guide you.'

I'm not very happy about this. The thing is, Frank can be a dick, but at least he's my mate and I pretty much trust him, whereas this voice is a new one. I'm being ordered about by all kinds of bloody bossy-boots at the minute. And come to think of it, where the hell has soft-voiced lass got to?

Despite serious misgivings, I push the door and squeeze in. When I let go, it closes again. There's a heavy old sideboard a couple of feet away that has left drag marks on the floor. It looks like someone has been moving it in front of this door to secure it. Right now it's not secured. I wonder how often this person comes here? I really don't like this. I glance around in the gloom. Although the windows are boarded up, there are tendrils of light creeping in through holes and gaps. It was obviously a pub once, though most of the furniture is gone. Just a few upturned chairs now. The bar is still intact, though of course it's booze-less. There's quite a lot of litter and detritus about the place, plus the smell of shit, and I wonder if it's been used as sleeping quarters by those with nowhere else to go? As I'm thinking this, my heart begins to pound. I'm scared, but also . . . what? Excited. There's something going on. Something big. I must go upstairs, that's what I'm being told. Go upstairs.

'I don't fucking want to go upstairs.'

'I will guide you.'

'Stop saying that, it's freaking me out.'

'I am with you.'

I doesn't matter – I can complain all I want, but I know I have to go up there, and my feet are already taking me to a door with a top half of glass, which looks onto a staircase. The door squeaks and the carpet on these stairs is minging. Brown and orange, with a lot of filth ground in, plus bare bits with broken wood from the smashed stairs, pointing up in all directions. There's light, as the huge window at the top of the stairs is opaque but not boarded. It does have two planks nailed across it, though, and the top pane in the arch is broken. There are doors. I peep through one and find myself looking down a hallway with two more doors off. Two of the upstairs flats, I'm guessing. This is where staff must have lived. Another door to the right probably leads to yet another flat, and there are more stairs up, this time with two doors at the top of them.

I go up and peek in the door to the left. It's a big office room, a total tip, with papers everywhere and a knackered-looking desk with a filing cupboard with no drawers next to it. The door on the right is sturdy-looking, with a big bolt, and when I push it across and open it, I'm looking onto a walled terrace. I step out into the waning early-evening sun and something jogs my memory. The terrace is about ten square feet of smooth concrete, with a wall about a foot shorter than me. Standing up, I can see a lot of Southwark – plus trains as they pass, I should wager. What's seriously messing with me, though, is the sofa. A dark-grey two-seater that's been out in all weathers for a long time, by the look of it. I feel it and it's dry. Tentatively I sit down, and now all I can see are buildings that are higher than this one, and the sky. I'm hidden from the trains and no one would ever know I was here. What a great spot to hide from the world. Also, I know this spot already . . . Why do I?

It hits me: walking up to Muswell Hill the other day, when I started to cry. The rush of emotions, the view of Southwark, then sitting on a sofa in the open air. Not wanting to die. Fuck me, it was here.

'Oh my GOD. Someone died here. Why have you brought me here?'

'It's time.'

And that's when the door behind me opens and out walks Stuart, the beggar, with his blanket around his shoulders. His hair is short and thick. He's carrying a two-litre half-finished bottle of cheap cider, and he stops in his tracks when he sees me jumping up from the sofa.

'Fucking hell, what are you doing up here?'

His voice isn't his friendly street-voice. It's the voice of a man who just found an intruder in his living room.

'Stuart! Hello. I'm sorry. I went for a walk after being at the graveyard, saw this place and thought it was a beautiful-looking building. I got a bit too nosy. I'll go . . .'

He stands between me and the door.

'You don't have to go, darlin'. I got a shock is all. Sit back down. It's a nice place.'

I don't want to sit back down.

'I really should be going, I need to get back to my, erm, boyfriend . . .'

Stuart smiles a yellow-toothed smile at me.

'I'm sure he can wait a little bit. Come and keep me company for a minute.'

He's staring at me. Assessing me. I wonder if my fiver bought him that cider? He adopts a conversational air, like this isn't weird in the slightest.

'Tell me why you were looking for Nelly. Did you find her?'

He sits on the settee and opens his bottle. I stand with my back against the wall, hoping that people can see me – see my neck and head. I want as many people as possible to spot me and know I was here. I have a very bad feeling. I can't believe that bloody voice brought me up here.

'Oh, I did, but I have some bad news. She collapsed today and died. That's why I was having a walk; it was awful.'

'Poor old Nelly.' Stuart lifts his bottle in the air in salute, then takes a swig. He offers it to me and I shake my head.

'No, thank you. I'm a wine girl.'

'Another one.'

'Another?'

He laughs to himself and looks at me. There's no smile in his eyes, though. Just pain.

'I used to know someone who loved her wine. She knew Nelly as well, actually. Her name was Jill.'

Oh, fuck! I decide to play dumb on this one. It might be a different Jill after all.

'Really? Who was Jill?'

'Jill was going out with a mate of mine, Per, who lived in the same flats as Nelly. I lived round the corner. Just before I got kicked out by my ex. I had a smoke with them sometimes. She was good fun, Jill. She used to call round to Nelly's for a cuppa and a chinwag as well, she told me. Felt sorry for the old bird. Nelly used to tell her all about her family. Sad stories apparently – a lot of them died and got buried in Cross Bones.'

'Yes. She told me.'

'Then Jill disappeared one night. No one knows what happened to her. Per was gutted, and Nelly lost her mate. Per moved away after the police made him feel like shit, like he did something wrong, and I . . . After my ex kicked me out, I started drinking a bit too much. And here I am ten years later. Living free!'

'You sleep here?'

His eyes narrow as he stares into his bottle.

'Not sleep, no. I come here to chill out. Once in a while I might flake out on this little sofa, but mostly I don't sleep.'

'You must be knackered.'

His laugh is loud when it comes.

'Good one! I am – I am knackered. Always knackered.'

He puts the bottle to his lips again, then glares at me.

'Did you really come here by accident?'

'Yes.'

'But, you see, no one knows about this place really, apart from one or two people like me. Everyone thinks it's completely boarded up and sealed.'

I think I should run for it soon, so I start edging closer to the door, pretending to admire the view as I reply.

'I know, strange, isn't it? I was wandering in a daze and

accidentally leaned against that door downstairs and it moved. I don't know why I got so nosy. I'm shocked it's just standing here empty, it's a lovely building.'

'It's been empty like this for years and years. Someone bought it, but they weren't allowed to do it out like they wanted, so it was put on the market again. It's been boarded up for about fourteen years. Doesn't even have security. It's changed hands so many times. Most of the derelict buildings around here have pain-in-the-arse security guards. When I was first slung out, I lived in here, put the hinges on the boards at the door. I cover it over when I'm in here, so other people can't get in'

'Yeah. I saw the big sideboard had moved.'

'You see a lot, don't you?'

I don't like how Stuart's friendly Yorkshire voice can turn so sinister at will. He's got a lot of anger in him, this lad. I can feel it radiating. I really need to leave now. As I think that, he jumps up and closes the door.

'Hope you're not thinking of going anywhere, darling. I want to tell you a secret.'

I don't want to know his fucking secret, I want to go home. He seems to have decided to confide in me, and I highly suspect this is a bad thing. I shout to Frank.

'Frank. He's dangerous. HELP ME!'

Nothing in response, which is not very comforting.

'Stuart, I'm running late now, and I watched someone die today; it was hellish. Could we maybe chat another time? I could take you for a coffee and some lunch maybe.'

'Yeah, like you'll be coming back to Southwark to see

me for lunch.' He stands and produces a small, but very sharp-looking knife.

My belly lurches. That's it, I'm fucked. I sit. He stands over me, Blade pointed at my face.

'I was good-looking, you know? Ten years ago I was twenty-nine and a handsome bastard. I liked a smoke and I liked a drink, but I was a good bloke. And people liked me, found me funny. My family were cunts, but I moved to London, got benefits, moved in with my ex, Dee, and was doing my music. I'm a good DJ, you know? And Per, he was an artist and we used to talk about shit 'til all hours. And Jill, when she came on the scene, she wasn't a pain in the arse like loads of women; she was funny and she liked staying up and talking, and she wasn't always nagging Per to get a job, go to bed at a proper time and all that. She liked who he was. She and Dee got on as well, but Dee wanted me to get a "normal" job and pay rent and all that. She was working, so it was bed at eleven and up at seven. She said I liked the sauce too much, but who doesn't like a drink when they're young, for fuck's sake? She needed to lighten up.'

He moves forward and sits by me, still gripping the knife while he takes a quick suck on his bottle.

'I think Dee must have got to Jill when she decided to throw me out, though. Said something about Per. Cos all at once Jill's saying that Per needs to get "some direction". They'd already said they didn't do marriage. They both said it, but this one night Jill asked him if he'd ever marry her, and he said no. So she walked out. I was wandering around, I'd been out on my arse for two nights, and I saw her coming out of the offie with some wine. I told her there was a great place we could go and talk, if she wanted to sort her head out. She said okay, and I brought her here. I'd dragged this settee out of one of the rooms and pulled it upstairs, and we sat and drank her wine. A bottle each. She told me she got depressed out of nowhere sometimes, and there were times she even wanted to die. Said she'd suddenly felt like it that week and she didn't know what to do. She said she didn't think Per was a "long-term option".

'It bothered me a bit, because Per loved her and she was saying pretty much what Dee had said to me. Fucking women, – you always have to be what they want. You can't be *you*. But still, Jill was looking so sad there and so pretty; she'd had her hair done all blonde and she was wearing a nice dress, and I'd had a bit of a skinful, so I put my arms round her and tried to kiss her. I thought if she and Per were through, maybe I could live with her instead. But Jill went weird and stood up and shouted.

'I was really scared someone would hear, so I grabbed her and pulled her back down and I tried again – just a kiss, that's all – then the next thing she slapped me, and I got mad, and suddenly she wasn't breathing any more and her face looked fucked. Black and ugly. I had no idea what had happened. And that's why I don't sleep much these days . . . I hide under my blanket and try to blot it out, but I still see her sometimes. She won't fucking leave me alone. This place didn't have a single visitor up them stairs for two years after that night except me, thank fuck. I made sure it was sealed tight with a massive lock. The flies were fucking everywhere. But now, all good. And yet I still can't fucking sleep.'

I feel sick. Of course I feel sick. I've already had to put up with Creepy Dan the Creepy Murderer, and now I'm with 'Stuart the Fucking Psychopath with a Blanket on His Head'. Why me? I look at the knife and I look at him.

'Stuart, I'm so sorry for what you've been through. Shouldn't you confess to the police? Wouldn't that help you sleep?'

He gives his big laugh again and has a drink.

'Don't be fucking stupid. I'm free. I couldn't survive being banged up. What good would it do anyone anyway, when she's been dead for ten fucking years? Why should I be punished? It was an accident.'

'Okay, well at least let me go. I haven't done anything.'

'Yes, you have. You came here. Somehow you knew. And now you can't leave.'

Shit, I'm so scared. But I'm pretty much determined this isn't my time to die. I'm about to direct Milo's play. I want to shag Neil again. My little mam will be mad enough that I got into this situation, without me actually dying while I'm consorting with spooks. Which reminds me: *spooks* have got me into this, and they don't seem to be getting me out. I am not happy.

'Frank. He's going to kill me.'

'*Jump up.*'

Oh, so now Frank's here.

'What?'

'*Jump up and to your right. When he jumps up after you, look at his balls. Then smack him right in the face with that brilliant right hook of yours.*'

I don't wait. I jump up and as I do so, Stuart, who is

faster than I expected, jumps with me. He's two feet away and his arm lifts and that knife comes straight at my face. Then stops dead, when a semi-solid Frank appears directly in front of me, nose-to-nose with Stuart.

Stuart screams like a terrified teenage girl, and Frank shouts, *'NOW.'*

I punch Stuart in the nose as hard as I can, straight through Frank's transparent form, and as he hits the deck, I begin to stamp up and down on his balls. I'm so furious and scared that it takes quite a few stomps before I stop. By now Stuart's too winded to scream again. Frank steps to the left and gives me the thumbs-up. Then I run to the door, rip it open and slam it behind me. I slide the big bolt into place. I can't see how Stuart will get through that, and I also can't believe what Frank just did – it was fantastic. I can't see him now, but I certainly hear him.

'I wouldn't have let him hurt you.'

'He came bloody close, though.'

'I was close. I was watching.'

'Thank you.'

'Now go through that door to the right.'

'Not straight downstairs? What if Stuart comes after me?'

'He can't, I promise. He's trapped there until someone lets him out.'

'Fucksake.' I go back into the office area. One of the windows isn't covered, so there's light. I hear that calm, androgynous voice again.

'Open the cupboard at the back.'

I sincerely don't want to open the cupboard at the back.

But I move quickly, as I can now hear weak banging from the door upstairs. The cupboard has a lock. Also, a shitty set of shelves has been put in front of the door to disguise it, but it's fooling no one. It's made of light metal and I knock it to one side.

The voice calmly informs me to look in the plant pot with no plant in it, behind me. There's a key. I put it in the lock and take a huge, deep breath. When the key enters the lock, I hear another flurry of bangs from upstairs and then silence. As I open the cupboard door, the silence feels like the whole building is holding its breath. I get the door wide enough to let light in. The cupboard is filled with ripped-up cardboard boxes and smells awful. Carefully I lift out handfuls of cardboard. Soon I reach long, highlighted hair. After a moment of catching my breath, I take out another box and see that the hair is attached to a mummified-looking skull and there are shoulders wrapped in a shitty blanket.

I don't go any further. I close the cupboard door and stagger towards the stairs. My knees won't work properly. Once I'm out of the side door and on the street, I hurry down to an open pub fifty steps away. I know I should scream and call the police immediately. But I ask for wine, sit down hard and hope Charlie answers as I press dial on my phone. He needs to know where his sister is and where her murderer is trapped, then bring the police in himself. He also needs to announce that he found his sister through an anonymous tip-off. I'm not going through a media circus like last time. Fuck that.

FUNKY FRANK, AND NELLY'S JUJU MAGIC

I called an Uber, paid a shedload and Sheila met me at my end. I was shaking like hell. She helped me get my key in the door, and now we're on the sofa. We have big mugs of peppermint tea, but I need something stronger. I'm clutching a beautiful big piece of Labradorite that I just found in a parcel from Gladys. I tell Sheila everything and she's very pissed off with me for doing it all without her.

'I think it had to be just me. I'm glad. If I'd put you in that much danger again, I'd feel even worse.'

'Why did you go into that boarded-up pub on your own, though, love? That was insane.'

'I know. I can't fucking stop shaking. I was told to go in by that extra voice, so I did. Frank was amazing, though.'

'Yeah, he sounds like he was bloody great. I think whatever Nelly was giving off certainly tuned you in more. Fancy finally seeing him in the flesh, so to speak.'

'I know. He was wearing a nice outfit as well – funky. He looked great.'

'I always look great. Now, close the blinds.'

'Oh, Sheila, he's here; he says to close the blinds.'

Sheila jumps up and closes them. The room is suddenly very gloomy. She sits beside me, and a light – like the one in the graveyard that heralded Oonah's arrival – begins to form in the middle of the room, five feet in front of us. Sheila's intake of breath is one of wonder.

'Oh, Tanz . . . how beautiful.'

Soon, iridescent and almost solid, stands a young woman with fair hair and twinkly eyes, wearing jeans and a kaftan shift, right there in front of us. With her face not blackened and her tongue in her mouth, she looks far less threatening than when she was standing in the dark in my hallway. She winks at me, the cheeky mare.

'Jill?'

'Hiya.'

Well, fuck me, the last piece falls into place.

'Oh my *God*, you're "soft-voiced lass". Why didn't you tell me?'

She looks a little sheepish.

'Nelly was throwing out her energy all over the shop. It was her time to leave, which had to be sorted out first, then I could put my brother and my parents out of their misery afterwards. I was being her friend still and guiding you. I'm so sorry you had to go through all that. Nelly lost the last of her marbles when I died, and she didn't know how to speak to the dead – only how to watch them in the past. But she did lead me to you, which meant we all got what we needed.'

'Apart from me. I didn't fucking need that heart attack

257

today, or the one last night, when you were zombieing around outside the door there.'

'*I wasn't zombieing. That was Nelly's superpower, finding the intense moments, linking into me as I died, with my face like a blackened turnip. You saw what she'd dug up. So to speak.*'

Jill starts to laugh and Sheila snickers, then suddenly we've all got the giggles.

'What was with the history lessons?'

'*Oh, Nelly told me all her stories and I started studying Southwark's history. Amazing, isn't it?*'

'Yes. But I'm sorry about what happened to you in Southwark, Jill.'

'*It's okay – I'm good. I wasn't good when it first happened; it took me time to adjust to being dead. But through you, my family will finally know the story, which is all I wanted. Plus, I'm an apprentice now. Learning all sorts of new skills through Frank. He hadn't left you to it, you know; he guards you all the time, he just doesn't always talk.*'

I feel my face flush and I fight the wobbly bottom lip at this.

'Well, that's nice to know. But who was that other voice? The one who took me to you?'

Jill glows brighter. She looks like a hologram of someone who's standing in a room lit by a strong white light. She's radiating happiness.

'*Oh, now that would be telling, wouldn't it? Suffice to say they're very impressed with you, and I'm sure you'll hear from them again. I want to thank you, Tanz. And thank you, Sheila, for being a wonderful teacher and friend to her. You both do very important work.'*

Sheila bows her head and grins.

'That's fine, love. I'm glad it's all sorted at your side.'

'It sure is. And I owe you one, Tanz. That's one in the bank.'

'Oooh, how exciting. What on earth can you get from the ghost bank? Incidentally, your brother gave me a photo of you with red hair – it threw me right off!'

'Yeah, sorry about that. I had it lightened two days before everything went to hell. Charlie showed you his favourite photo, the daftie.'

Suddenly there's a light beside her and, to my amazement, Frank appears, still looking funky. I'm not sure my heart can take much more today. I would give anything for a hug off him right now and I start to blubber.

'Oh my God, what's wrong with you?'

'I miss you.'

'This again?'

He laughs.

'You'll never get rid of me, you dope. Well done for tonight, that must have been scary – sorry you had to go through it.'

I can't speak. The day has finished me off. Frank moves forward and leans towards my cheek. I feel a warmth, as if he's kissed me, and I swear I smell him. That makes me sob even more.

'I love you, Frank.'

'I love you too, you soft ninny. Look, we have to go. I

just wanted to drop in quickly while you're still seeing us so solidly. Lovely to meet you, Sheila.'

'Lovely to meet you, Frank. You're better-looking than I realized – no wonder she's crying.'

I slap her arm. Frank nods to Jill, then smiles at me again.

'I'll speak to you soon, you daft cow. I won't be able to appear to you like this all the time, once Nelly's juju magic wears off, mind you.'

Jill waggles her fingers at us.

'Thank you for everything, Tanz. Getting a proper look at you, I'd say you're definitely more Cher than Susan Sarandon.'

And, just like that, they disappear.

We both sit there, me with a runny nose and wet eyes, Sheila grinning about the latest ghost parade. I'm mulling over the fact that Jill has been my right-hand woman through this whole thing and I hadn't a clue who it was. What a strange life.

It's getting very dark out there, so instead of opening the blinds, Sheila switches on the lamps and, as she does so, my phone lights up and I remember that I turned the ringer off. It's Neil.

'Do you mind if I get this, Sheila? It's Neil.'

'Of course not.'

I answer. 'Hello?'

'Fucking hell, woman, are you insane? You could have been killed. Are you all right?'

'Yes, I am. I'm home now.'

'Charlie called me. He thinks you're a super-witch, and I just needed to know you're okay. He says he's tried to ring you, but you're not answering the phone. Can I . . . can I come over and cuddle you for the night? Make sure you're safe?'

Christ on a bike, I've never had a better offer.

'Yes, please, I'd like that.'

EPILOGUE

Message from my little mam. Left for me on my phone when it was on silent, and I was breaking into a boarded-up pub in Southwark.

'*Tanz!* I bloody knew it. You and your "It's not dangerous, Mam, it's only a graveyard, Mam . . ." I just went upstairs to put the ironing away and I suddenly saw a bloody great skull with long hair on it, floating over my dressing table. Well, I dropped the lot, didn't I? All that ironing in a pile on the floor. You stop messing with them ghosts *right now*. There's something dangerous going on and if I find out you're mixed up in it, there'll be hell to pay. Call me back as soon as you get this message. Worrying me sick. I've got enough going on with your nanna, without all this. You ring me back, young lady. But try to make it after *EastEnders*. Bye, love. Bye now. Bye.'

I'm still too scared to call her back.

ACKNOWLEDGEMENTS

Writing this book was such an intense labour of love. I wanted to honour the Winchester Geese, the poor people of Southwark who were badly treated in death, and the many, many Irish folk who showed up to escape a preventable, disgraceful horror at home, just to walk slap-bang into another one. I'm eternally grateful to Wayne Brookes and the team at Pan Macmillan who liked this book almost as much as I did, plus I'm ridiculously indebted to the tornado of kind, efficient brilliance that is Lucy Hale.

I also want to thank everyone who offered support as I beavered away, writing all day every day, wondering if this was the novel that would finally get me a brilliant publisher (it did). In no particular order: Lee Mattinson, Lee Proud, Ahd Tamimi, Violet Fenn, Ali Lee, Karen and Paul Burgess, Lainey Shaw, Trevor Wood, Roz Wyllie, Sinead Skinner, Lee Morgan, Kate and Jack Deam, Ralph and Ali Ineson, Sarah Shafi, Daniel Brennan, Helen Wyatt, my

N10 posse, my Taproom heroes, my Gateshead besties, my family. Everyone who cheered me on, while I wondered if I'd finally 'get there' writing about a subject that set my heart on fire. Thank you all.

THE ACCIDENTAL MEDIUM

Tanz is a wine-loving, straight-talking, once-successful TV actress from Gateshead, whose career has shrivelled like an antique walnut. She is still grieving for her friend Frank, who died in a car crash three years ago, and she has to find a normal job in London to fund her cocktail habit.

When she starts work in a 'New Age' shop, Tanz suddenly discovers that the voices she's hearing in her head are not just her imagination working overtime, but are in fact messages from beyond the grave. Alarmed, she confronts her little mam and discovers she is from a long line of psychic mediums.

Despite an exciting new avenue of life opening up to Tanz, darkness isn't far away – all too soon there's murder in the air.

GIN PALACE

Tanz can talk to ghosts, although she'd prefer it if she couldn't. Struggling to make ends meet as an actress and wholly unsuited to supply teaching, Tanz is only one bad day away from a meltdown. And the babbling ghosts aren't helping.

So when Tanz is offered a paid acting gig in her hometown, things start to look up. But Newcastle's dead won't stay quiet for long, and soon Tanz becomes haunted with visions of a mysterious Gin Palace guarded by a sinister figure. As Tanz starts to piece together a terrible tragedy, it becomes clear there's no limit to what the poltergeist will do to keep his secrets his own.

Unfortunately, he's never met anyone quite like Tanz before . . .